Return of the Cowgirl

Return of the Cowgirl

The Gallaghers of Montana Romance

Eve Gaddy

TULE
PUBLISHING

Dedication

This is for Justine Davis. Thanks so much for listening, emailing, and helping me figure out what the heck I was going to do about my amnesiac cowgirl.:)

And for Janet Justiss who told me to send Glenna to Argentina several books back and I listened to her. Janet, why Argentina?<g>

Dear Reader,

Finally, the missing sister's story.

Sometimes I'll have a character in one of my books and I don't know what to do with him or her. It's usually a member of the family I've been writing about for several books. Return of the Cowgirl is the missing Gallagher's story. Glenna is the only girl in a family of five siblings, four of them brothers.

I didn't know what her story was so I sent her off to Argentina to work on a horse ranch. And kind of forgot about her. Oh, I'd remember occasionally, which is how she came to be suspected of embezzling. And how she disappeared. And then I'd wonder why the heck I did that. It's known as writing yourself into a corner.

So I started Return of the Cowgirl knowing a few things. But I still didn't know her story. It wasn't easy to figure out her story but once I did I had a lot of fun. My title for it is The Amnesiac Cowgirl. For some reason Tule wouldn't let me have that title.<g> But that's how I'll think of her forever.

Her hero, Mitch Hardeman, was also fun to write. He's the PI who finds her and eventually brings her back to Marietta. Not without a lot of problems, not the least of which are his growing feelings for her.

I hope you enjoy Glenna and Mitch's story as much as I enjoyed writing it.

Eve

Chapter One

S HE SAT AT a small table in an outdoor café in Valparaiso, Chile, a battered backpack at her feet. She looked as lost and alone as anyone he'd ever seen. Mitch Hardeman walked up to her table and said, "You are a damned hard woman to find."

"*No entiendo,*" she said, her expression changing to annoyance. And oddly, alarm.

Bullshit, you don't understand. But if that's the way she wanted to play it, fine. "*Vos sos una maldita mujer dura para encontrar,*" he repeated in Spanish.

"You must have me confused with someone else. I have no idea who you are or what you're talking about," she said, still in Spanish.

He didn't mind speaking Spanish, although he didn't know why she was pretending to not understand English. "You don't know me, but I know you, Glenna. My name is Mitch Hardeman. I'm the private investigator your brothers hired to find you."

"My name is not Glenna and I have no brothers. Go

away or I will call the waiter to remove you."

Instead of leaving, he pulled out a chair and sat, signaling a waitress. When the woman came over, Mitch ordered coffee for two. He lifted a brow at Glenna to see how she'd react but she simply shrugged and turned away. For a moment he wondered if he'd made a mistake, but even though this woman had brown hair instead of dark red, he knew she was the woman he'd been chasing for the better part of three weeks.

She didn't stand out as American—he'd give her that. With dark hair, a smattering of freckles and green eyes, and wearing a dress with tiny flowers on it, she looked as much like a native as anyone. She sure as hell spoke Spanish like a native, but then, she'd been living in Argentina for years.

He tried again. "Your brothers have been looking for you since they discovered you vanished from the Villareal Ranch several weeks ago."

"Brothers? I told you I have no brothers and I know nothing of this ranch you speak of. Go away," she repeated.

Mitch pulled out the picture of Glenna Gallagher he carried with him and showed it to her. He had digital photos as well, but it was often easier to show people a paper photo. "Are you trying to tell me this isn't you? You aren't Glenna Gallagher?"

She looked at the picture and paled. "That is not my name, no. So go away. Now."

The waitress returned with their coffee. *NotGlenna* took

hers with a thank you and sipped. Her color had come back and she seemed to have collected herself. Apparently growing tired of Mitch ignoring her requests for him to go the hell away, she got up, slung her backpack over one shoulder, and without a word started walking off.

Mitch threw some money on the table, picked up the picture and followed her, catching up to her a short distance from the café. "Other than your hair, you're the spitting image of the woman in this picture. So stop it with the denials. I know good and well you're Glenna Gallagher."

Glaring at him, she said, "My name is Rosalie Torres."

This was why he'd lost her just after Zapala. She'd changed her name, dyed her hair and disappeared. Again. She was worried about her previous employer tracking her down. Otherwise, why the phony identity? But if she really had embezzled fifty thousand bucks, then what the hell was she still doing in South America? She should have been long gone by now.

Her brothers maintained she hadn't done it. They were convinced that wasn't the whole story and that their sister would have never stolen anything, much less fifty thousand bucks. He wasn't so sure, but after meeting her employer, Jorge Villareal, and his son, Rolando, Mitch leaned more toward believing her innocent.

The men—especially the younger man—hadn't been any more forthcoming with Mitch than they had with Dylan Gallagher when he'd talked to them. They'd flat-out lied to

Dylan about how long Glenna had been gone. As to why they lied, all he could think of was to make them think there was no point in looking for her. They wanted nothing to do with Mitch, and were clearly angry that he'd come looking for their errant employee. They did ask him to let them know if he found her.

Yeah, that wasn't happening. Not too long after he left the ranch and continued his search he figured out someone else was looking for her, and had been for a while. Probably since she'd disappeared. Villareal's flunkies seemed the most logical conclusion.

So while he kept up his own enquiries, he was able to catch up with them pretty quickly. All he'd had to do was show Glenna's picture around and ask if someone else had been looking for her.

He wasn't sure how she'd managed to evade them for so long. She was clearly smart and resourceful. And desperate?

That's the feeling he got. So how could he get her to admit she was Glenna Gallagher?

"Are you afraid the Villareals are looking for you?"

She looked at him blankly. Really blankly. As if she had no clue to what he was referring. "The Villareal Ranch?" he prodded. "You know, the place you lived and worked at for the last seven years? Until you were accused of embezzlement?"

"Embezzlement? You're crazy. I'm not this Glenda person. Must I call the police so you'll leave me alone?"

This was not going how he'd envisioned it. Did she think he was on the Villareals' payroll? Maybe she didn't believe he came from her brothers. Or...could he be wrong? What if she really wasn't Glenna but simply looked enough like her to be her twin? Except for the hair, of course. But hair color was easily changed. He tried one more time. "Glenna, not Glenda. Do the names Jack, Sean, Wyatt and Dylan Gallagher mean anything to you?"

He watched her closely but didn't see a glimmer of recognition. Nothing to indicate she'd ever even heard of the four men who were her brothers.

Instead of answering, she ducked into a store, one of those selling everything from fabric to antiques. Crammed full of merchandise as well as people, it was an effective place to lose someone. But not Mitch.

She ran out the back door and Mitch followed, only a minute or two behind her. He burst out the door just in time to see a man grab her and drag her, fighting madly, toward a beat-up van waiting in the street.

Holy shit, she's being abducted.

Chapter Two

ROSALIE SCREAMED AND the man clamped a filthy hand over her mouth. She bit him, heard him curse as he yanked his hand away and let go of her for a moment, long enough for her to turn to face him. She kicked him in the nuts, then swung her backpack at his head but he threw up his arm to deflect it. She ran then, but not fast enough. He grabbed her blouse, ripping it as she struggled wildly. Then his hands were around her neck and her vision started to blur. Just before she went under, he dropped his hands.

Collapsed on the sidewalk she watched as the man who had harassed her earlier fought with her would-be captor.

Get up! Run! She got to her knees but as she tried to stand, a wave of dizziness hit her and she fell back down. Painfully, she crawled over to the wall, dragging her backpack along with her, and prayed her rescuer would prevail.

The sickening sounds of flesh striking flesh and explosive curses from the men were glaringly loud in the silence of the deserted street. Someone shouted "*¡Policía!*" The two men continued to struggle until her kidnapper broke away and ran to the waiting van. They were gone in an instant.

Bleeding from his mouth and his nose, her rescuer came over and squatted beside her. "Are you okay?"

She nodded. Her knees hurt from crawling on the concrete, and she suspected they were bleeding, but thanks to this man she wasn't bound, drugged and being sold as a sex slave. There had been a rash of abductions, she'd been told, that most people put down to human trafficking.

And there was always the fear that whoever she was running from had found her.

A policeman was coming their way and she fought a surge of panic. She didn't know why; she only knew it was the same feeling that came over her whenever she saw a policeman. The same feeling that drove her to move from town to town, never staying long in one place. The same feeling that made her dye her hair brown, instead of leaving it her natural color. A redhead would attract too much attention. Clearly she'd thought so, judging from the red roots she'd seen when she first awakened in the hospital. She grabbed the man's arm and said hoarsely, "No police."

"Why? You were nearly abducted. Don't you want to report it?"

How could she explain when she didn't understand it herself? "No. Please. Get rid of him."

He stared at her a moment, then shook his head. He pulled up his shirt and used it to wipe at the blood on his face. Then he stopped the policeman a few feet away and she heard him explaining they didn't want any trouble and his wife—*his wife*—was all right.

A wave of dizziness swept over her and she put her hands to her head. She heard voices, hers and a man's, arguing.

"*Why did you say we were engaged? We've never discussed marriage.*"

"*Querida, what is this? Of course we're getting married. It is time for me to have an heir.*"

She came back to herself and stared at the policeman. What had he said? "¿Perdón?

He repeated, "¿*Es verdad? ¿Está bien?*"

"*Sí. Sí. Estoy bien, gracias.*"

Rosalie waited until the policeman left before saying, "Your wife? Really?"

"You're welcome. Do you want to tell me why you were almost abducted? And oh, yeah, why we're speaking Spanish again when you were speaking perfectly good English before you talked to the cop?"

Rosalie started to deny it, then realized that he was right. "I—I can speak English?"

He stared at her. "What the hell are you playing at? Of course you speak English. You're as American as I am."

"American? No, no. I am Argentine."

Wasn't she?

SHE DOESN'T KNOW she speaks English. Honestly doesn't know she's American. What the fuck? Either Glenna was a superb actress or this woman wasn't his quarry. But she spoke English. And she looked like the picture. With red hair she'd look *exactly* like the picture. He knew in his gut she was Glenna Gallagher. If he was right, why the hell did she keep denying it?

Maybe she doesn't know. Oh, right. Maybe she has amnesia. Because that was such a reasonable thing to think.

No, it was more likely she still thought he was with the Villareals. Except if he was, why would someone else have tried to abduct her? Why wouldn't he have just snatched her himself?

Whatever, he had to convince her that her brothers had sent him. The easiest way to do that was to put her on the phone with one of her brothers.

Realizing Glenna was trying to get up, he held out a hand and hauled her up. Her neck already showed signs of being choked. "We should get you to a clinic," he said in English.

She answered him slowly, as if still unsure of her language skills. "No. I'll be all right. Thank you, but you can leave now."

Fat chance, honey. "Let me walk you home. In case those losers come back."

"No."

Definite. And scared. "Fair enough. You don't know me. Let me at least walk you closer to where you live."

She didn't answer but started walking. He noticed she

was limping. She'd banged herself up good crawling on the concrete.

"Do you know who tried to kidnap you?" He was nearly certain it had been the Villareals' henchmen. There was a slight chance it was a random kidnapping, but that seemed unlikely as hell, given the situation.

"No. Not...exactly." Hesitantly, she added in Spanish, "But someone has been trying to find me. And I can't let them."

"I've been trying to find you. I've been all over South America looking for you."

"No." She shook her head. "It's not you." Casting him a suspicious glance, she said, "But until you rescued me from those men, I wasn't sure of that."

But she still didn't trust him, and honestly, why the hell should she? "Can we go somewhere and talk? In public," he added hastily.

She looked at him for a moment and said, "Come with me."

She took him to the *Plaza Sotomayor*, an open-air plaza in the middle of the city's Historic District. They found an unoccupied bench and sat. She arranged her skirt to cover her knees but not before he saw that they were rubbed raw and bleeding.

"Are you sure you won't go to a clinic?"

Ignoring his question she asked one of her own. "Why do you think I'm this woman, Glenna?"

"Like I said, I've been chasing you all over South America for nearly three weeks. From a couple of weeks after you left the Villareal ranch to now. You look exactly like this picture, except you have brown hair, which is easy enough to change." He took out his phone as he spoke and pulled up a digital photo of Glenna Gallagher. He showed it to her. A different pose than the paper copy.

He couldn't tell what she was thinking, but she hadn't shut him down, at least. "What I don't get is why you keep denying you're Glenna. What's the point of that? I can see why you want nothing to do with the Villareals, given they accused you of embezzlement, and it's extremely likely that your kidnappers are connected to them. But your family is totally on your side. Are you afraid I'm lying about them?"

While he talked, she searched for something in her backpack. "I've told you I don't know what you're talking about. Or who you're talking about." She pulled out her passport and handed it to him. "Look at it."

He opened it. *Rosalie Maria Torres.* Nationality: Argentine Place of birth: *La Pampa Province,* ARG. The passport picture looked like her, more or less. The passport itself was marginal at best. Mitch had seen his share of fake passports and he'd bet his ass that this one was fake.

"Nice try, but this is a fake," he said, handing it back to her.

"It isn't fake," she insisted. She handed him her DNI card.

"Also fake," he said, adding, "The quality is better in this than the passport, though."

"You're wrong. You have to be wrong."

Mitch opened her passport and pointed out the things that made him suspect it was phony—besides the fact that he knew she was Glenna Gallagher. Then he did the same with the National ID card.

She appeared stunned, staring down at the paperwork in her hands. "These are not…not authentic?"

"Afraid not."

"Then…who am I?"

Chapter Three

MITCH STARED AT her as if she were crazy. Perhaps she was. Her world, such as it was, was rapidly crumbling. Everything she knew about herself since the accident was, apparently, a lie. And she still didn't know who she was hiding from. Only that it was necessary to hide. Was Mitch right and she'd been running from a charge of embezzlement all this time?

"Who *are* you? What the hell does that mean? Don't you know?"

She'd trusted him this far. And he *had* saved her from those men, who clearly meant her harm, whoever they were. Maybe she really was Glenna Gallagher. She hadn't known she spoke English. And her hair wasn't naturally brown. She knew that for a fact. "No, I don't. I don't remember anything before I woke up in a hospital near Zapala a few weeks ago."

"You have amnesia? Amnesia? You've got to be fu— freaking kidding me."

"Unfortunately, I'm not. I woke up in a small hospital in

Argentina. I was told I'd been in a bus crash." And that she'd lost her baby. A baby she hadn't known she was carrying. Although, as she had been at least five months along, maybe a bit more, she must have known it before she suffered the amnesia. "I had my backpack with a few clothes, my passport, and my DNI card in it. What money I had was in a hidden pocket of my jeans."

"You woke up speaking Spanish?"

"That's what everyone spoke. I understood it and had no reason to speak another language."

"Amnesia," he muttered in a disgusted tone. "Goddamn amnesia."

"You don't believe me."

"I don't know." He scrubbed his hands over his face. "It would explain a lot of things I've been wondering about. Your hair—"

"I put a brown rinse on it. It's red. Like the woman in the picture."

"Why? If you thought you were Rosalie Torres and everything was on the up and up, why did you color your hair and why did you continue moving around? Why go to Chile, for that matter?"

If he didn't believe she had amnesia he sure as hell wouldn't believe the rest of it. "Never mind that. You answer some questions for me. Why should I believe I'm this Glenna person?"

He took his phone from her and keyed in something. A

picture came up and he magged it up and handed the phone to her. "That's your brother Dylan with his horses at the Gallagher ranch. The local paper—the *Copper Mountain Courier*—did a spread on him and his operation some time ago."

She studied the picture. He was a nice-looking man. A cowboy with dark hair and an engaging grin. And she didn't recognize a thing about him. Handing the phone back, she shook her head. "I'm sorry."

Mitch pulled up several more pictures, taken at different events in Marietta, Montana. The Christmas ball, various charity events, the Copper Mountain Rodeo—he pulled them all up on the Internet. He showed her all four of her supposed brothers. Not a glimmer of recognition pierced the veil in her mind.

The veil that sharply divided the time before the accident and afterward. She remembered almost nothing of her life before. Nothing but an occasional flash or a fragment of a memory. Nothing except fear and the knowledge that she was being hunted. Even so she couldn't be completely certain of that, only that the fear was so strong she'd acted on that feeling. And judging by the fact that if it weren't for this man sitting beside her she'd have been kidnapped, she'd been right.

She was on the run. Running for her life?

"WHO ARE YOU calling?" Glenna asked Mitch.

"Your brother Dylan. We'll see if he can convince you of your real identity."

"You believe I have amnesia?"

He studied her for a long moment, his fingers hovering over the phone. "If you don't then you're a damn good actress."

She didn't answer. Mitch finished punching in the number.

"I found her," he said, and immediately lost the call. He tried texting but he couldn't get that to go through either. "Great. Fucking great," he muttered.

"Come on," he said to Glenna. "I need to be someplace with better reception." They walked around the square and the adjacent streets until he found a café with free Wi-Fi. "This should do it."

This time it rang through and Dylan answered immediately. "Where are you? I tried to call you back but I couldn't get it to go through. Where's Glenna? I want to talk to her."

"First you need to listen to me. We've got a problem."

"What kind of a problem? Is Glenna hurt?"

"Not exactly."

"What the hell does that mean? I swear to God, Hardeman, if you—"

Mitch cut him off. The sooner he told him what he thought, the better. "I'm convinced she's Glenna, but she isn't." He glanced at her, nervously biting her lip.

"Come again?"

"The woman I believe is your sister has amnesia."

There was a long silence. "You're shitting me," Dylan Gallagher said flatly.

"Yeah, I know how it sounds. It's a long story and I'll fill you in on it later, but in the meantime I'd like you to talk with her and see if that helps her remember something. So far she can't recall a thing before she was in a bus accident a few weeks ago. She doesn't know whether to believe me or not. I had a hell of a time getting this far with her. If you recognize her voice that would help, too." He handed her the phone.

"Hello," she said hesitantly. "Who am I speaking to?" She was quiet a moment, then said, "You're the rancher. The others are doctors. According to Mitch." Another pause.

Mitch wished he'd put it on speakerphone but he was afraid their voices might not be as clear or easily recognized. He didn't know if Dylan recognized her, but it was pretty damn obvious she didn't recognize him.

"No. I'm sorry. None of that sounds familiar." She handed Mitch the phone. "He wants to talk to you."

He took it back. "Yeah," he said grimly. "She didn't recognize your voice."

"She didn't know anything I told her. But it's Glenna. It's her voice."

Glenna got up, motioning to the back of the restaurant. She probably just wanted to use the restroom, but given what happened earlier he wasn't about to let her out of his sight. He followed, still talking to Dylan.

"Does she have any scars, distinguishing characteristics? Something hidden, that I can't see? I'm not sure she's buying what I'm telling her."

"She has freckles."

"So do lots of people."

"Her hair is a really pretty shade of dark red."

"It's brown right now. Tell me something that's hidden."

"She doesn't have any birthmarks. Maybe—Wait, I've got it. High up on her right leg she has a scar from a barbed wire fence."

"Ouch. How did she get that?"

"We were about twelve and thirteen. We went riding, bareback. Glenna wore shorts. She took a fall and ran into a barbed wire fence. It wasn't pretty."

"Riding bareback in shorts?"

"We were young and not very bright."

Mitch gave a crack of laughter. "Okay, I'll try that. Let me call you back later when I'm not loitering by the women's restroom. I'm getting funny looks and besides, the reception is spotty where I'm standing."

"I don't suppose we could video chat? It might help her to see me. Or my brothers."

"One, I don't have the app on my phone. Two, the reception isn't good enough here. Three, I doubt she'd go for it. She's pretty skittish." He frowned and rubbed his nose.

"But once I can get her to my hotel I'll convince her to try and we'll use my computer."

"Damn it. Okay. When should I expect your call?"

"Not for a while. First, I need to convince her who she is and then, when we've had a chance to figure out our next move, I'll call. There's more to the story," he said, thinking of her would-be kidnappers. "I'll text you first to see if you can talk."

"All right."

Mitch could tell he wasn't happy but the last thing he needed was to be dealing with finding good reception to call the States. "Don't worry, I'll take care of her."

"You'd better. Tell Glenna we miss her and we love her."

"Will do." He hung up and knocked on the bathroom door. "Glenna?"

"I'm Rosalie and I'm busy."

"Do you have a scar on your right leg?"

She yanked open the door and glared at him. "What?"

"Dylan says you have a scar from a barbed wire fence, high up on your right leg."

She rolled her eyes and shut the door in his face. A minute or so later she reopened the door. Her expression was odd. A mixture of emotions, all battling for dominance.

"Well?"

"I have a scar. I don't know what it's from."

"Is it where Dylan said it was?"

"Yes. But it could still be a coincidence."

"Unlikely. Dylan said he recognized your voice." She still looked unsure. "Do you want me to look at it? I've seen barbed wire scars before."

"You just want to look at my legs."

Mitch laughed. "Don't worry, honey. I've seen legs before. Your virtue is safe with me. You're not my type."

The hell she's not. She's young, beautiful and smart enough to evade the Villareals' men for weeks. She's a goddamn damsel in distress. But her luck could be coming to an end. In fact, it might have ended today if I hadn't managed to stop the snatch. She's exactly the kind of woman who could get me into real trouble.

"Well?" she asked sharply.

Mitch realized she'd pulled up her dress on one side, high enough to show the scar. He stared at the scar, doing his best not to run his gaze over the rest of her very shapely leg, and failing.

"Looks like barbed wire to me."

She's a job.

Right. Keep telling yourself that.

Chapter Four

THEY LEFT THE café and started walking, heading in the general direction of her hostel, though she didn't tell Mitch that.

"What now?" Mitch asked. "Is it sinking in that you really are Glenna Gallagher?"

Sort of. The scar had shaken her, as well as going a long way toward convincing her of the truth of Mitch's claim that she was Glenna. She'd felt a twinge of—not recognition, but something—when she talked to Dylan. He'd certainly talked to her as if she were his sister. He'd sounded sincere, and disappointed, though trying not to be, that she didn't remember him. It still felt odd to be talking in English when she hadn't even known she spoke it until a few hours ago.

A lot had happened since a ridiculously hot man had plopped himself down at her table early that morning and begun spinning an impossible story. *A story that seems more and more likely to be true.*

She looked at Mitch. Should she trust him? He seemed determined to hang around. Honestly, though she'd tried to get rid of him, the kidnapping attempt made her grateful for his company. "I don't know. Maybe." She sucked in a breath. "What do you suggest we do now?"

"I think we should get out of here. The city and the country. I'd like to take you back to Marietta. Will you let me?"

"If I had the money I'd already be out of South America. Aside from that, even if I had money, how am I supposed to get into the United States? According to you, my passport is fake and not very good."

"Are you sure your real one is gone? Maybe you hid it somewhere."

"I don't know where." She patted her backpack. "Everything I have is in this backpack, and there's damn little of it."

"Can I look at your backpack? Maybe it's in there and you don't know it."

"Like a secret compartment?" she asked skeptically.

"Exactly." When she remained silent he said, "Is there anything I can do to prove to you I don't mean you any harm? That all I want is to take you back to your family?"

Oh, hell. If she refused he'd just follow her and right now she didn't feel up to evading him. Her throat hurt, her knees were raw and painful, and she had a mother of a headache. She stopped walking. "All right."

"All right, what? What does that mean?"

"I'll let you look at my backpack and we can discuss what to do. But first I need a *farmacia*."

"We can still go to a clinic. I noticed your knees were bloody when you showed me your scar." He raised a hand and very gently touched her throat. She flinched away. "That has to hurt like hell."

"It does," she snapped. "Which is another reason I need a *farmacia*."

"Or a clinic," Mitch repeated.

"*Farmacia*," she said firmly.

They started walking again. "How much money do you have?" Mitch asked.

"Very little." Barely enough to pay for the cheapest hostel she could find. "Not enough to buy an airplane ticket."

"Don't worry about that. Your brothers will take care of tickets."

"It doesn't feel right, taking money from people I don't know."

"But they know you. Dylan said to tell you they love you and miss you."

She wished she could remember. It would be nice to have a family. She turned onto a narrow street lined with cobblestones. The buildings and houses had been getting progressively shabbier and more neglected the longer they walked. The hostel she'd found wasn't a big step up from a hovel, but it was cheap and that was her main concern.

"This is where you're staying?" Mitch eyed it with distaste.

"Yes." She raised her chin and met his eyes with a challenge in hers. "I can't afford a more expensive place. It's hard to find temporary work, especially for only a week or two." Work that didn't involve selling her body, anyway.

AFTER STOPPING AT the pharmacy for bandages and antiseptic ointment—which Mitch had to fight her to pay for, they headed for her hostel. Mitch followed Glenna to her room: a bunk in the co-ed dormitory of the *Casa En La Colina* hostel. The *House on the Hill* was better on the inside than it looked on the outside, thank God. She was clearly low on funds, but she'd been traveling around South America for weeks now, so that wasn't a big surprise. Another point in favor of her not being a thief. If she'd had the money she'd supposedly embezzled, she sure as hell wouldn't stay in a place like this.

No, if the Villareals wanted her, and he had to think they did, then they wanted her for another reason. But what? Glenna didn't know. Hell, she didn't know her name, much less why she was hiding from the Villareals. Or, as unlikely as it seemed, hiding from someone else. Maybe if they talked about it something would come back to her.

The dorm room was empty except for the two of them. Glenna sat on the bed, told him to have a seat and dumped the contents of the backpack onto the bed. "I leave my clothes and a few toiletries here but the rest I carry with me. Not that there's much."

Mitch sorted through the items on the bed. Pitifully little. Two fake IDs, a hairbrush, a small spiral notebook and pen, a candy bar that had seen better days and a local paper with jobs wanted ads. "No wallet?" he asked. "Where's your money?"

"In a pouch I wear around my waist. Or in an inside pocket of my jeans when I wear them. Otherwise there's a high chance it will get stolen."

Mitch inspected the bag carefully. Opened every pouch. Checked the stitching for irregularities. He hit pay dirt on the inside bottom of the main compartment. He pulled out his pocketknife and carefully began to pick apart the seam.

"Remember, it's the only one I have. Are you going to sew it back together when you finish?"

He shot her a look. "I can't sew. I'll buy some glue. Better yet, I'll buy you a new one."

"I don't want your charity."

"It's not from me. It's from your family."

"Same thing."

He stopped picking at the stitching and looked at her. Her mouth—damn, a mouth made for kissing—had a stubborn set to it. No fucking way was this woman a thief. Mitch was intimately acquainted with more than one dishonest woman. Rosalie Torres/Glenna Gallagher didn't fit the mold. He tried to soften his tone.

"It's not charity. Your family loves you and wants to help you. They want you to come to Marietta." She pouted. A

25

damn sexy pout. *Shit, stop thinking about her mouth, you moron. She's a job.*

"It's charity, whatever way you look at it. I pay my own way."

"I can respect that. But you don't have any money, unless you've got some stashed in this backpack. Looks to me like you have a choice. Accept the help and get out of the country, or stay in Chile and wait for someone to try to snatch you again. It's up to you." He left that for her to think about and went back to his task.

After a long pause she started talking again. "I'm paying them back."

"Take that up with your family when you get there." He had a feeling there'd be a fight about that, but that was for the Gallaghers to work out between them.

One of her roommates came in just then and after a brief discussion in Spanish with Glenna, he gathered together clothes and a towel and left for the common bathroom. As soon as he was out of the room Mitch said, "We won't be able to catch a flight tonight. First we have to either find your real passport or go to the embassy and get you a new one. In the meantime, let's go to my hotel. It's a lot more comfortable than this place."

"You go. I'll stay here until you've worked out something definite."

"That's not happening," he said flatly. "Are you forgetting about your friends from this morning? Those two fine, upstanding citizens the Villareals sent after you? You're a sitting duck here by yourself."

"We don't know for certain they were from the Villareals," she protested.

"Maybe not, but there's a damn good chance they were. In which case they're still looking for you and it's only a matter of time before they find you again." He touched the bruises on her neck. "Next time you might not be so lucky." Especially if she was alone.

"Maybe they were sex traffickers. It happens."

"It's possible but it's damned unlikely. Three different sets of people pursuing you? That's a bit much. Besides, you don't remember, but you've been hiding from the Villareals since you left the ranch. Come with me, Glenna. I have a room in a decent hotel with a lock on the door. Nobody's getting past me to hurt you. You'll be safe there until I can get you out of the country."

She gazed into his eyes, trying to decide whether to trust him this last step, he suspected. Her eyes were a rich, deep, emerald green, with dark eyelashes he'd bet were natural. He doubted she'd worn makeup at least since she'd left the hospital, maybe longer.

Even bruised and battered, with dyed hair, and unsure of her identity, Glenna Gallagher was a beautiful woman. One he'd do well to remember was simply a job. "What do you say? Are you ready to get out of here?"

Chapter Five

MAKE UP YOUR *mind. Trust him or don't but get off the damn fence.* He had an honest face. His eyes weren't shifty. They met hers squarely, with a hint of amusement. At the moment she'd call them hazel, but really they were undecided, as if they couldn't make up their mind between blue, green and gray. He was a good-looking man, tall and broad-shouldered without an ounce of fat on him. He looked to be in his mid-thirties. A few years older than her, although she only had a fake ID to tell her what her age was. She'd have to ask Mitch how old Glenna was.

Honestly, she didn't have much of a choice. Whoever was looking for her had almost certainly found her once. And since they had, it wouldn't be hard to find her again, especially if she stayed in Valparaiso. Whether she was running from her former employers or someone else, she was just about done in.

As for Mitch, if he planned to do something awful with her, why hadn't he done it? Why the elaborate story about her family and her previous employment—including that she'd been accused of embezzling, for God's sake—if it wasn't true? If he'd wanted to coerce her for some nefarious purpose he'd had ample opportunity. Instead, he'd saved her from God knows what kind of horror.

Her gut said to trust him. Even before he'd come to her defense, she hadn't gotten a bad vibe from him. Merely an annoying one.

"How many beds are there?" she asked.

"One. But there's a sleeper sofa."

It would be nice to have her own room, but she didn't want to owe the Gallaghers any more than she already did. Plus, she doubted he'd go for it since he had decided she needed protection. The hell of it was, he was probably right. After all, he'd foiled a kidnapping attempt only this morning. "All right."

"Good. I'm going to wait on further inspection of the backpack until we get to my hotel." He closed his pocketknife, tucked it into his pocket, and handed her the pack.

"Let me get my stuff together and we can go."

It didn't take long to pack up her things. She was traveling light, to say the least. Her belongings consisted of some clothes, a few toiletries, a beat-up pair of running shoes, and the stuff on the bed that he'd dumped out of her backpack. When she finished she grabbed her jacket hanging on a chair back, and slung the bag over one shoulder. "I'm ready."

"You've got everything?"

"Every bit of it."

Mitch opened the door and waved her through. On the way out she ran into her roommate and told him she was leaving.

He looked at Mitch and then at her. "*¿Estás seguro?*"

"*Sí, gracias.*"

"He's looking out for you," Mitch said as they walked away.

"Miguel is a nice guy. He thinks of me as a sister."

Mitch raised an eyebrow. "A sister? Not likely."

Ignoring his comment, she went to the desk and told them she was leaving. She'd paid for a week's stay but since she only had one night to go, she didn't haggle for any money back. It wasn't worth it when she knew they wouldn't go for it.

They walked back to one of the more traveled streets and Mitch hailed a taxi. *God, I'm tired,* she thought as she got in the cab and relaxed.

The next thing she knew, she woke with her head on Mitch's shoulder and him saying, "We're here."

Still groggy, she followed him inside and up to his room. It wasn't fancy but it was miles above anything she'd stayed in since she woke in the hospital in Argentina with no memory and very little money. Spacious, with a queen bed and a sofa, just as he'd promised. And a bathroom. With a bathtub.

"Oh, my God."

"What's wrong?"

"Nothing's wrong. If you want to use that bathroom you'd better do it now. When I get in there I'm not coming out for at least an hour."

He laughed but took her at her word and went into the bathroom. He came out a short time later, wiping his face with a towel. "There's no room service but there's a café in the hotel. Or we can go out."

"Here is fine." She took her backpack with her into the bathroom, shut and locked the door, turned on the taps and began to strip.

NOW IS AS good a time as any to call the Gallaghers, Mitch thought. He knew they'd be anxious to hear from him, even if he couldn't give them a definite idea of when he could bring Glenna back. He couldn't make airline reservations until they sorted out whether Glenna had a real passport or not. He wasn't at all interested in trying to sneak her into the US with the fake passport.

He texted Dylan and got a reply right away, so he called.

"When are you coming back?" Dylan asked as he answered the phone.

"I don't know. Could be as few as a couple of days, but that's only if we find her real passport. Otherwise we'll have to go to the Embassy for a replacement and that could take awhile."

"Has she remembered anything yet?"

"No, but I think she's just about accepted she really is Glenna Gallagher and not Rosalie Torres."

"Where are you?"

"At my hotel. She was staying at a hostel and I convinced her to come with me."

"Where's Glenna? Can I talk to her?"

"She's taking a bath." He chuckled, remembering her face when she'd spied the bathroom. "Said she wasn't coming out for an hour. We can arrange a time to video chat if you want."

"I do want, but in the meantime fill me in on everything."

Mitch went through the whole story, which took awhile. Dylan asked a few questions and made a few comments, such as wanting to kill the would-be kidnappers, but mostly he let Mitch talk and didn't interrupt.

"How sure are you that the Villareals are behind the kidnappers?" he asked when Mitch had finished.

"Ninety-five percent. I know for a fact they were looking for her at first. I followed them until Zapala. That's where I lost them and Glenna. If I hadn't heard about the bus crash by chance, I'd still be looking for her."

"Why are they looking for her if they don't have enough evidence to charge her with embezzlement?"

"That I don't know. Neither does she, obviously. But even with amnesia, she's convinced someone is after her." They talked a bit more, arranged a time for a video chat and

Mitch hung up. Twenty minutes later Glenna emerged from the bathroom.

At least, he thought it was Glenna. His tongue stuck to the roof of his mouth. *Holy shit. I thought she was pretty as a brunette but as a redhead she's a stunner.*

"What's wrong? Why are you staring at me like that?"

"Your hair…it's red."

"Well, duh. It's red in the pictures you have. Assuming I'm Glenna, of course. I decided I could wash out the rinse I put on it." Her expression grew worried. "Was that a mistake? Should I color it again?"

"It's, uh, memorable." Hot damn, was it memorable. A rich, dark red and flowing well past her shoulders, it was the kind of hair a man wanted to wrap his hands in while he— *Shit! Shit, shit, shit. You really are a moron, Hardeman.*

"Oh. I thought since we were leaving the country it wouldn't matter."

Speaking of shit, Mitch finally managed to get his together. "We are, but I'm not sure how long that will take. Do you have a scarf or something you can cover your hair with?"

"No. My wardrobe doesn't run to scarves," she said dryly.

"We'll have to buy you one. There's a shop next door. But in the meantime, try this." He went to his bag, pulled out a ball cap and handed it to her.

Frowning, she took it and went back in the bathroom.

When she came out she'd managed to stuff her hair beneath the cap. "How's this?"

He could still see some of it, but at least it wasn't hanging out in all its glory. "It'll work until we get you a scarf."

Glenna picked up her backpack and slung it over a shoulder. "I'm ready when you are."

Unfortunately for him, she was still beautiful. And he had no business at all thinking about what she'd taste like if he kissed her.

Chapter Six

*T*HAT WAS WEIRD, Glenna thought, following Mitch out of the hotel. *He couldn't get out of there fast enough.* He'd been tongue-tied when she first came out of the bathroom.

Which was odd because he didn't seem like the kind of guy to let much of anything faze him.

She recognized the look in his eyes, even though he'd masked it quickly. Appreciation. From a man who'd said she wasn't his type. And why the hell was she wondering what Mitch thought of her? Whether he was attracted to her or not?

Because you think he's hot.

And so what if he was? The last thing she needed was to get involved, however briefly, with a man. Any man. Much less this man she was depending on to get her out of Chile and get her…home?

She was sure part of the attraction was because she had nothing to hold on to. It was all well and good to have other people be sure she was Glenna Gallagher, and that she had a home and a family in Marietta, Montana. But she couldn't *feel* it. It still wasn't real to her. But Mitch was very real. Solid. Strong. Dependable. And, yes, damn it, hot.

"This place should have scarves," Mitch said. "And why don't you get something else to wear while you're at it?"

"Because I'm not spending any more of their money than I have to."

Mitch rolled his eyes. "Has it occurred to you that the fact you are wearing the same things over and over makes it easier to find you?"

Crap. No, it really hadn't. "Fine. I'll look for something else to wear."

Mitch said nothing, just let her go ahead of him through the door. The shop was tiny but crammed full with all sorts of wares. She looked for a scarf first, thinking that unless she colored her hair again, which she was really tired of doing, that was the first and most important thing she needed.

She found a large, brightly colored scarf that she would have loved to have, but since it screamed 'look at me' she put it back. Picking out a muddy brown and dark green scarf, she showed it to Mitch. "What about this?"

He looked very much the bodyguard, his arms crossed over his chest as he leaned back against a convenient post, sharp eyes taking in the scene and watching the entrance. He looked at the scarf she held and snorted with disgust. "It's ugly. Really ugly."

"But very unobtrusive."

He shrugged. "You have a point."

Glenna picked out a gauzy scarf to go around her neck and hide the bruises, found a pair of slacks that looked about her size, then a long-sleeve shirt and a flowing shirt to go over it. All in dark colors. Boring, but she ought to blend in with any group of people.

As she started to take her things to the shopkeeper, Mitch stopped her. "You need a coat or a jacket too."

"Why? This is a blue jean jacket," she said, waving a hand at the one she had on. "Everyone has them."

"There's no point in doing it half-assed. Get a different jacket," he reiterated.

Grumbling, she thrust everything, including her backpack, into his arms and went back to look for a coat. Picking up a black jacket, she carried it with her to where Mitch waited with her other items. They piled everything in front of a wizened older man who looked them over and named a ridiculous price. Mitch started to get out his money but she stopped him.

"Absolutely not," she told him. Haggling was something she'd learned well since she left the hospital. With so little money, she'd had no choice but to learn. She and the shopkeeper haggled until he refused to go lower.

"Come on," she told Mitch in Spanish. "We're going somewhere else, to someone who won't try to rob us." When they reached the door the old man called them back. Grudgingly, he agreed to her price. "Okay, you can pay him," she told Mitch.

Triumphantly, she left with her purchases. "Why are you laughing?" she asked Mitch.

"You drive a hard bargain."

"It helps not to have any money."

He sobered. "You almost certainly have money in a bank account here."

"Maybe. But I have no idea how to access it. Besides which, if I'm under suspicion of embezzling they've probably frozen my account."

"I'm sure your family will help with that when you get home."

"What if I'm not her?" What if he and the Gallaghers were doing all this for a stranger? How would they feel then?

He put his hand on her arm to stop her. "Look at me." She met his gaze. "You are Glenna Gallagher. I'm sure of it, and so is your brother, Dylan. We arranged to have a video chat later. Dylan will be able to see you and you'll see him. Maybe that will bring back your memory."

"What if it doesn't?"

"Then you'll just have to trust Dylan until it does."

IT AMAZED MITCH that with just a few changes Glenna looked like a completely different person. She was still pretty. He didn't think it would be possible to take that away from her. But with her hair covered by an ugly scarf, another scarf, almost as ugly, around her neck, wearing brown slacks and a shapeless shirt that came to mid-thigh, she wasn't at all noticeable.

Then she smiled. *Damn, she'd better not do that very often.*

"You're staring at me," Glenna said.

"Sorry. You look different."

"I thought that was the point."

"It is."

"Because you think the Villareals are still after me."

"I think they're looking for you, yes. I'm hoping you won't be easy to find." He let her precede him into the hotel restaurant. "The food is decent here," he said as they were seated and the hostess handed them menus. "The empanadas are really good, if you like them."

"I do." She glanced at the menu, then set it aside. "That's what I'll have then. Beef empanadas."

"Two beef empanadas," he told the waitress when she greeted them. "Do you want a glass of wine?"

"No, but you go ahead."

"Not for me either. *Solamente agua, por favor,*" he told the waitress.

"I don't know how much I can drink without it going to my head," Glenna said. "And since my head is already screwed up, I think it's better not to drink."

"Wise decision."

"I've been thinking about something. What if I really did embezzle that money? What if I'm a thief?"

He couldn't help smiling. "Somehow I doubt that a woman who argues about buying a few clothes because she doesn't want to spend someone else's money is guilty of embezzling." Even if he hadn't been certain she was Glenna Gallagher, he wouldn't believe she was a thief.

"But you can't know that for sure. What if the Villareals have a legitimate reason for wanting to find me?"

"If they're legit why did they lie to your brothers? They weren't pleased that their ranch was my first stop. And why did they attempt kidnapping? Why not go to the authorities?"

"I don't know. But we're still not certain the Villareals were behind that."

"Maybe not certain but it's pretty damned likely. As for why they didn't go to the authorities, I'll tell you why. Because they claimed they didn't have proof, only suspicions. Which in itself is suspicious." He thought about that a moment. "I met Jorge—he's the father—when I first got to the ranch. I talked to him a little, but I mainly dealt with Rolando, the son. The old man is afraid of the son. He tried to hide it, but his son scares the crap out of him. There's something off about Rolando Villareal. I think he's the motivating force trying to find you, but I'm not sure that has anything to do with embezzling. I think there's something going on at the ranch. Something Rolando doesn't want anyone to know. Maybe something criminal."

"Why?"

"For one thing their successful cattle ranch isn't so successful. From what I found out their cattle business is on its last legs. Yet you wouldn't know they had a money care in the world."

The waitress brought their food and they both began eating. "This is good," Glenna said. "I'm glad you suggested it." She took a few more bites, set down her fork and asked, "What makes you think they don't have money problems?"

"Two Ferraris and a Porsche." He took another bite of food and washed it down with water.

Glenna stared at him open-mouthed. "*Two* Ferraris and a—"

"Porsche. Yes."

"I wonder…if I am Glenna…what do I know about that?"

"Whatever you know, I don't think they want you talking about it."

"I would imagine not." They finished eating but before they left the table, she asked Mitch, "What if they're looking for me because I'm the one who screwed up? Maybe I didn't embezzle, but what if I'm the one who ran the cattle business into the ground? I was in charge. I was the manager. Maybe they started a criminal operation and they blame me for needing to do it."

He hesitated, not wanting to lie, but not wanting her to take the blame for something that might have been no fault of hers. "We won't know what really happened until you regain your memory. But after my visit with the Villareals I had my secretary do some research. The ranch was making a big profit, particularly the cattle business, until about a year ago. The decline was sudden and then the disease killing so many of the stock pretty much sealed its fate. Was that your fault? Maybe. But maybe not. So my advice is to try not to think about that until we have some facts to go with the speculation."

"There's nothing I can do anyway, except feel like a failure. Maybe that's why I hadn't talked to my family in so long."

"There's no sense torturing yourself with what-ifs." Except that's what she was doing.

Glenna said, "Mitch? There could be yet another reason they're looking for me."

"I'm listening."

"When I was at the hospital they told me I lost the baby. I said 'what baby?' They said I'd been about five months along when they brought me in from the bus accident. So I not only lost my memory, I lost a child as well."

He covered her hand with his. "I'm sorry. That must have been terrible."

"I'm sure it would have been if I could remember it. But obviously, since I don't remember the pregnancy, or the miscarriage, or much of anything before waking up in the hospital, I have no idea who the father was either."

Realizing he still held her hand, he hastily let go of it.

"That puts a whole new light on things, doesn't it? I wonder if Rolando was the father?"

"He could have been. Again, assuming I'm Glenna. Even if he was, I don't think we were married."

"Why is that?"

"I didn't have a ring, or a tan line from a ring. And…" She hesitated, then said, "I don't feel like I'm married."

"Why would you remember being married if you don't remember anything else?" It shocked him how much he wanted her to be right—that she wasn't married. Married to a man who was very likely a criminal, if not at least complicit in a crime. Because regardless of what was going on at that ranch, attempted kidnapping was for damn sure a crime.

"I don't know. It just seems like I would."

"Neither Villareal mentioned you being married. I don't know why they wouldn't say so if you were."

She brightened. "Yes, you'd think they would have said that first thing. So I don't have to worry about being married. If I'm Glenna. But if I knew I was pregnant, and it seems like I would have, why did I run away?"

"Because you were accused of embezzling."

"With no proof, you said." She sighed. "Or because I screwed up. I have a horrible feeling it's my fault the cattle business failed."

"If it was your fault I don't believe you'd have skipped."

"Why not?"

"Because you're not the type to cut and run."

She shrugged, as if she didn't believe him.

"I think to really know what happened we're going to have to wait until you regain your memory," he repeated. If she did. He was going to talk to Austin as soon as he got back to the States. His brother was a neurologist. He should know something about amnesia and how to treat it.

Mitch checked the time on his phone. "It's almost time to video chat with Dylan. Are you up for that?"

"I guess. It still feels weird."

"I'm sure it does. But maybe it will help."

"Maybe."

She didn't sound too sure and, frankly, neither was he. But it was worth a try, and besides, Dylan and the rest of her family were really anxious to see her.

Chapter Seven

"WE'VE STILL GOT some time before we're supposed to call your family. Let's finish looking in your backpack," Mitch said when they got back to his room. "I think there's a false bottom."

"All right. Let me empty it out." Glenna had mixed emotions about talking—video chatting—with the Gallaghers. She couldn't help thinking that they could all be mistaken and she wasn't Glenna Gallagher. Then what the hell would she do?

Mitch would go back to looking for the real Glenna. He wouldn't kick her out tonight, though. He wouldn't be that cruel. Even if she wasn't Glenna, she was still a woman who'd lost her memory.

"Can I ask you something?" She stopped emptying the backpack.

"Sure. What?"

"If it turns out I'm not Glenna—"

"It won't," Mitch interrupted.

"If I'm not—" she continued "—do you think the Gallaghers would consider lending me the money to get to the States and letting me work it off? I'd be willing to do whatever they needed. Not that I know exactly what I can—"

"Stop. Just stop." Mitch grasped her arms gently. "Look at me." She met his gaze and he continued. "You are Glenna Gallagher. I'm sure of it. But even if you aren't, I am not leaving you here. We'll figure out the details later. Not that it's going to be necessary. Got it?"

She nodded, and said around the lump in her throat, "Thank you."

"Don't thank me," he said brusquely, letting go of her. He pulled out his pocketknife. "Let me have your backpack."

She sat cross-legged on the couch and watched him work on the lining of her backpack. She started to say something but Mitch gave her the evil eye so she didn't. He worked in silence for a while and then said, "Hot damn. I was right. There's a false bottom."

"What?" Leaning forward, she bumped heads with him. "Ouch."

He rubbed his head. "A little anxious, are you?"

"Try terrified."

"Go ahead. It's your backpack," he said, handing it to her.

She pulled the false bottom out the rest of the way. There was a packet of something wrapped in plastic and strapping tape. Saying nothing, Mitch handed her his pocketknife. Carefully, she cut through the tape and pulled aside the plastic. The first thing she saw was money, two packets of it. A lot of money, maybe? She put it aside until she had everything out. Beneath the money she found a passport and a DNI card. Her heart was beating so fast she was afraid it would burst out of her chest. Turning over the DNI card, she stared at it. The picture wasn't great but it looked like her. Glenna Leigh Gallagher. Silently, she passed it to Mitch and opened the passport. The picture was better and the name the same. Glenna Leigh Gallagher.

"Is this where I say I told you so?"

She burst into tears.

HELL, HE HATED women crying. Nothing made him feel more uncomfortable. He didn't know how to comfort her so he did the only thing he could think of. He put his arm around her and hugged her. Comfort her, right. He didn't even know why she was crying.

She turned in to him, buried her head in his chest and sobbed.

Oh, fuck. What do I do now?

She was an incredibly sweet armful, even sobbing. He put his other arm around her and patted her back. Looked down at the top of her head, at all that thick, beautiful dark red hair, so long it fell down her back nearly to her butt. Her hair was soft and silky beneath his hands, and he wanted to bury his hands in it, tug her head back and—

Goddamn it, get hold of yourself, you fool.

"Glenna." She continued to cry. "Glenna," he said more firmly. Holy shit, she was about to descend into a crying jag. "Stop crying. Everything's going to be okay." Well, except that she'd lost her baby, her memory, and the bad guys were probably still after her. But hey, at least she had a real passport now.

"I'm sorry," she mumbled into his chest. "I shouldn't… I can't…" She drew in a wavering breath and sniffed. Then she raised her head and gazed at him with tear-drenched emerald green eyes. "I can't even say I'm not usually like this because for all I know—" she sniffed again and continued "—I cry all the time."

He smiled. "I doubt it. You've had a hell of a day. It started out with some man you didn't know accosting you and telling you that you were a woman you'd never heard of. Then you were nearly abducted. And that's just for starters." He touched the bruises on her neck gently. "I bet those still hurt."

"Kind of."

Her mouth was so close. Her lips were full and tempting. Right there, begging to be kissed. Still gazing at him, she moistened her lips. He managed not to groan, somehow. One of her hands rested on his chest, the other was at his waist, where she'd been holding him. Clutching him as if he were a lifeline. God, he wanted to kiss her. Just a taste of that sweet, sweet mouth.

What the hell was he doing?

Abruptly he let her go and stood up. "How much money do you have there?"

She stared at him a moment, looking, he could have sworn, disappointed. Because he hadn't kissed her?

Dream on, dumbshit.

Glenna shrugged. "I don't know. It looks like a lot."

He picked up one of the two stacks of bills and flipped through it, then did the same with the other. "Hundreds and fifties. Quite a few hundreds and fifties. A stack of each, in fact." A half-inch thick bank stack, which, if it was what it looked like, meant one hundred of each bill. However, the bands weren't as tight as they should be, which he took to mean some of those bills were missing.

"So I did embezzle the money."

"No, I don't think so. There's nowhere near fifty K here. And besides, embezzling is usually done electronically. But this is about fourteen or fifteen thousand."

She simply stared at him. "I've been carrying around *fifteen thousand dollars cash* in my backpack? Are you freaking kidding me?"

Her voice had gone higher, shock registering in it. He had to smile at her astonishment.

"No. But I have a feeling everything isn't on the up and up with these bills."

"What does that mean?"

"Think about it. That's a shitload of cash for you to be walking around with. Do the Villareals keep that much cash

49

around?"

"How the hell would I know?" she snapped.

"I think it's unlikely. Unless it's money from a drug deal. Or a bank robbery. Or it could be arms or even human trafficking." Another thought occurred to him. South America, particularly Peru, was known for excellent counterfeiting of US dollars. But counterfeiting wasn't unheard of anywhere in South America. What if the Villareals decided to invest in a counterfeiting operation rather than another illegal activity?

Mitch pulled out a bill from each stack and held them up to the light. First the hundred, then the fifty. He looked for the telltale signs that the money wasn't legit. He'd become familiar with counterfeiting during his many trips to South America. "These are good. Really good. But I'm about ninety-five percent sure they're fake."

"Fake? You mean they're counterfeit? I have fifteen thousand dollars in counterfeit money? Damn it, I could be thrown in jail forever."

"Calm down. That depends on why you have it. Come here." He didn't tell her yet that he believed she'd spent some of it. He held the hundred up and showed her a couple of reasons why he thought the bills were counterfeit. "I think this started out as a Venezuelan ten-bolivar note. They're worth very little—about two cents apiece—so they can get them cheap, bleach out the picture and put Ben Franklin's on it. In the US the security strip is red and blue. On this

RETURN OF THE COWGIRL

one it's lilac-colored. But the paper is real, so they're hard to detect."

"Okay, say you're right and it's phony. Why do I have it if I wasn't going to spend it?"

"I think you did spend some of it. Fake IDs and passports cost money. I won't know for sure until I've counted it, but if these are bundled as bank stacks, some of what should be there is missing."

He grabbed his laptop, took it to the couch, and booted it up. Ignoring the numerous unread emails, he started with googling bank robberies in Argentina. Not finding what he looked for there, he googled arrests for illegal arms sales, human trafficking and counterfeiting in Argentina, especially near the Villareal ranch. He struck pay dirt with an article about counterfeit bills being found in a couple of the larger cities near the ranch.

Clearly impatient with his computer searches, Glenna asked, "Do you think this is what the Villareals want? The money?"

"I don't know. But I'd hazard a good guess that it is. I wonder how you came by this money? I doubt they left it lying around."

"I wouldn't know," she said with a snap of annoyance. "Maybe I was part of the operation."

He gave her a sharp look. "No, you weren't. Not voluntarily, anyway. But you could be married and your husband was careless because he trusted you." He did not want to think about Glenna being a part of a counterfeiting ring. Or that she was married to a scumbag criminal, either. "Maybe you'll remember it."

She snorted. "Since I haven't remembered jackshit yet, not even about the baby they said I lost, I'm not going to hold my breath."

"There might be something you could do to help regain your memory. When we get to Marietta you should go see my brother."

"Why?"

"He's a neurologist. He might be able to help you. Austin Hardeman is his name."

"I'm sure I don't have insurance. Certainly not in America. According to you, I've been living in South America for years. And I don't have any money, either. Other than a crapload of what we assume is counterfeit money."

"I'm willing to bet you had the bills to expose the Villareals' counterfeiting operation. But since you were in hiding from them you didn't have a chance to give it to the authorities. Or possibly, you were too scared to go to the local police. Which makes sense. Then came the bus accident."

"And I don't remember anything about any of this," she said in disgust. "Unbelievable."

He wanted to help her.

You are helping her. You're taking her back to her family, his practical side reminded him.

Her family who are strangers to her, his you-never-learn side said.

Everyone is a stranger to her.

Everyone except me.

She could be married. To a criminal.

Which is exactly why she needs my help. She needs to get the hell out of here.

You're hopeless, Mr. Practical said.

Hopeless? No, he damn sure wasn't. Nuh-uh. Nope. No fucking way. Not doing that again.

But it wasn't an act with Glenna. She really did have amnesia. She wasn't playing him. Still, he'd learned the hard way not to let his sympathy overtake his common sense.

Sympathy? Is that what you're calling it? You've got the hots for her, man. Remember what happens when you think with your dick.

Chapter Eight

"WHAT HAPPENS NOW?"

Mitch looked at his phone for the time. "Right now, we need to video chat with your family."

Her family. People she didn't know. But they knew her. They would expect things from her. Things she couldn't give. "I don't want to. It's only going to make all of us feel bad. Because I can't remember them. Do we have to call?"

"No one is forcing you to do it, Glenna."

"But you think I should."

"All of your brothers are anxious to see you. They've been looking for you for a long time. They haven't heard from you in even longer. It will really help them to see you."

"I don't know them. What am I going to say?"

"They know you have amnesia. Three of them are doctors. They'll understand. They won't push you."

Glenna drew in a deep breath. "Make the call." She might as well get it over with. Besides, they were paying for her to fly out of South America. The least she could do was thank them.

And there was a faint hope—very faint, in her opinion—that seeing her four brothers together might jog her memory. She listened as Mitch called them.

"Hardeman, it's about time."

"Sorry. Something came up. I'll tell you about it later."

"Is Glenna all right?"

"She's fine. Still doesn't remember anything but an occasional fragment from before the accident."

"Damn, I guess that's not a surprise."

"No. Let me put Glenna on. Do you want to sit here?" Mitch got up, gesturing at the desk chair.

Mitch was going to think she was the biggest weenie ever, but she didn't care. Clutching his arm, she said in a low voice, "Don't go. Please."

"They're your family," he said quietly. "They love you. You don't need to worry."

"None of this feels real. Except you."

Something flared in his eyes but she couldn't say what sort of emotion it was. He gazed into her eyes as if trying to read something. But she knew the only things he'd see were anxiety and bewilderment. "I'll sit on the bed, right behind you. I won't leave."

"Thank you." She sat down and looked at the computer. Four good-looking men—two with dark hair, one with blond, and one with brown—looked at her with varying degrees of hope.

"Hello."

"Hi, Glenna. I'm Dylan," one of the men with dark brown hair said.

"Hi, I'm Wyatt," the blond said.

"And I'm Jack. It's good to see you," the other dark-haired man said.

"I'm Sean," said the man with sandy brown hair. "You look a bit overwhelmed. We won't keep you long."

"I am," she said, glad at least one of them understood her feelings. "I'm sorry. I don't recognize any of you."

"Don't worry about it," Dylan said. "We get it."

"We just wanted to see you," Sean said.

"And now that we have," Jack said, "we'll let you go."

"Bye, now," Wyatt said. "Take care and we'll see you soon. Can you put Mitch back on?"

"Yes," she said with relief. "He's right here." She remembered she'd wanted to thank them. "Thank you for buying my ticket back to the States. I'd like to pay you back." *Somehow.*

"That's not necessary," Jack said. "We'll talk about it when we see you."

"All right. Goodbye."

"Are you okay?" Mitch asked in a low voice. He searched her eyes. "Never mind. I'll be off in a minute."

She nodded, went into the bathroom, shut the door and buried her face in her hands. *Oh, my God. I didn't recognize one single thing about them. How can they be my brothers when I remember nothing?*

"WHAT'S GOING ON, Hardeman?" Jack asked. "Bring us up to date."

"Yes, and tell us about your plane reservations," Dylan said.

"All right, but it's a long story. Glenna's in the bathroom, so let me talk and then you can ask questions. Do they know about what I told you earlier?" he asked Dylan.

"Yes. Go ahead."

"I think we've found why the Villareals are after her." He wasn't going to tell them about Glenna's pregnancy and miscarriage. That was for her to tell. Unless he discovered it was important for them to know and even then, he'd try to convince Glenna to talk before he said anything. "This is still at the speculation stage, but I think Glenna discovered that her employers had started running a counterfeiting business. Making US dollars." He went on to tell them about the money they'd found.

"The hell you say."

"Yes. Their cattle business went to shit. And to top that off, their herd was decimated by disease. I'm not sure which of those came first. At any rate, they tried an alternate stream of revenue."

"You're sure about that?"

"Given their lifestyle, yeah, they have to have another source of income."

"How do you know the money is counterfeit?"

"I've had some experience with counterfeit bills. It's counterfeit." He continued, telling them everything in more detail. When he finished, they all started firing questions at once. "Hold it," Mitch said. "One question at a time." They didn't look happy but they shut up.

"What are you going to do with the money?" Jack asked.

"I think it would be best to take the fake money and dump it in the local authorities' lap. They can deal with the US. I don't want to take Glenna back to Argentina. We don't know if the authorities there will believe her, not to mention, there's still the matter of the embezzling accusation and the fact that I believe the Villareals are still after her. I want to get this evidence into someone else's hands as soon as possible. The sooner I get her out of South America the better."

"That's for damn sure. Considering she was almost kidnapped earlier today."

Was it only this morning that had happened? It seemed like much longer ago.

"When is your flight?" Wyatt asked.

"I haven't made reservations yet. I'll try to arrange them tonight, but the airlines require at least twenty-four hours to check our passport numbers. During that time we'll go to the authorities. I'll text Dylan the details when I have them."

"Take care of her."

"Don't worry. I will." He clicked off and shut his computer, but left it running. He'd get busy on the reservations as soon as he checked on Glenna. She still hadn't come out of the bathroom. Mitch knocked on the door. "Are you okay?"

"No."

"What's wrong?" *Dumb question.*

She yanked open the door and he almost fell into the bathroom. "Gee, I don't know. Maybe I'm upset because I can't remember a goddamn thing about my life before a few weeks ago. I don't remember my brothers. I don't remember the US, much less a ranch in Marietta, Montana. I didn't even remember that I spoke English, for God's sake, until you started speaking it to me. The only person I know in the whole damn world is you, and you obviously can't wait to be rid of me. So, no, I'm not upset. Nothing at all is wrong!" Her voice rose until she was practically shouting the last words.

"I don't want to get rid of you." Which was a stupid thing to say, considering everything her tirade had entailed.

"You don't?"

"No. I'm trying to protect you, and the best way to do that is to get you out of the country."

She gave a choked-off laugh. "I'd say I don't need protecting but that would be a big fat lie." She pushed past him into the bedroom. "I'm sorry I got hysterical. I don't usual-ly—Oh, shit, I have no idea if I do or don't. There I go again."

"Why this orgy of self-castigation?"

"That's not what I'm doing."

"Seems like it to me. Look, give yourself a break. A lot of shitty things have happened to you in a very short time, not the least of which is you lost your memory. Of course you're feeling bewildered and confused. Anyone would."

She crossed her arms over her chest and raised her chin pugnaciously. "I don't like it."

"Yeah, I get that. Do you want to talk about it?" Not that he could think of much to say to make her feel better. Even at the best of times he wasn't any good at talking.

She shrugged. "Not really. I pretty much said it all during my hissy fit. And don't deny that's what it was."

He smiled. "I wasn't going to." She looked exhausted. Exhausted and beat down. He didn't think that was her usual manner. "Get some sleep. You can have the bed. Things will look better in the morning."

"No, I'm not taking the bed. I'll be fine on the couch."

He shrugged. "Whatever you say. I'm going to see about plane reservations."

She went back in the bathroom with her backpack and came out wearing flannel pants and a T-shirt. He'd pulled out the sleeper bed while she was gone and tossed a pillow on it.

"Mitch? What do we do now? About the counterfeit money? Give it to the police in Argentina? Do I have to go back there?"

She got in bed and pulled up the covers. All he could see

was her hair and part of her face. "No, I don't want you anywhere near Argentina. Tomorrow morning we'll take the fake bills to the local authorities. They can get in contact with the proper US authorities. Likely the Secret Service."

"The Secret Service? That's who handles counterfeiting? Really?"

"Yes. They have an anti-counterfeiting department. There could be an office in Santiago, but I think the sooner you get this evidence out of your possession, the better."

"But the Villareals won't know that I've given it to the authorities?"

"If the Argentine police can tie it to them and raid their operation they will."

"Mitch?"

"Yeah."

"Why do you think I remember things like the Secret Service but I can't remember my brothers?"

He looked up from the computer and rubbed the back of his neck. "I don't know much about amnesia but from what I've read, memory is quirky like that. In most cases, most of your memories come back. It just takes time."

She was quiet a moment, then asked, "What if they don't?"

Chapter Nine

G LENNA ROSE UP on her arm to see Mitch's reaction. Not that she believed he'd have a solution but she was going crazy wondering if her life would ever return to "normal" and what in the hell normal was for her.

He sighed and turned his chair to face her. "The first thing you do is stop thinking of every worst-case scenario. There's no reason to believe you won't get your memory back eventually."

"There's no reason to believe I will, either."

"Damn, Glenna, you're just going to have to take some things on faith. Stop working yourself into a frenzy over something you don't have any control over."

Glenna flung herself back on the bed. "I hate not having control."

"Don't we all," he muttered. "I need to make these reservations. The sooner I make them the sooner we can get out of Chile."

"And you want me to shut up."

His only answer was a *hmm*. Glenna sat up again and

saw he'd turned back to the computer. Since he wasn't paying attention to her, she let her gaze roam over him. He was hot, no doubt about it. Early to mid-thirties, medium length dark hair, hazel eyes, a strong jaw and the beginnings of stubble, not to mention the gun residing in the back holster, made him look dark, dangerous and sexy. He wore jeans and a T-shirt that showed off sleekly muscled arms and a hard, manly chest. She bet there were some serious muscles there, too.

She hadn't intended to throw herself on his chest and cry, but he'd handled it surprisingly well. Apparently, she wasn't afraid of men because having Mitch hold her while she cried had only made her want to snuggle against him more. He was very, very comforting. Dependable, though why she was so sure of that when they'd only met this morning baffled her.

He saved you from the kidnappers, stupid.

Oh, yeah. But hell, besides that, he really was the only person in the world who she knew right now. Not that she knew much about him. "Are you married?"

He grunted. "I'm working here."

"So you are married. What's she like?"

"What's who like?" He turned his head to stare at her.

"Your wife."

"I'm not married."

"Ever been married?"

He heaved an exasperated sigh. "Can we postpone the

twenty questions until after I've booked our flight?"

"If you promise to talk to me and not blow me off."

"Fine. I promise. Now be quiet."

She knew she should go to sleep, but she couldn't. Her mind was racing and she couldn't shut it off. She tossed and turned and pounded on her pillow, but none of it helped. She considered turning on the TV but if Mitch didn't want her talking to him, he probably wouldn't go for the TV either.

Finally, he shut down his computer, turned the bedside table lamp on low, set his gun beside the lamp, and laid his shoulder holster over a chair. He went into the bathroom and when he came out he'd taken off everything except his jeans. His chest was even better than she'd imagined and the washboard abs didn't hurt a bit either.

What was she doing, ogling the guy? *Trying to forget about all the other shit, that's what.*

He turned off the light and got in bed. All without saying a word.

"I'm not asleep," she announced.

"I could be if you'd be quiet."

"You said you'd talk to me when you finished booking our flight. Did everything go all right?"

"We should be on a flight to Miami leaving day after tomorrow. So we've got one day and a night to get your evidence to the local cops."

"Good. You never answered my question. Have you ever

been married?"

"Yes. A long time ago. Now go to sleep."

"Did she break your heart?" she asked, ignoring him.

He gave a crack of laughter. "Yeah, you could say that."

"What happened?"

"If I tell you will you shut up and go to sleep?"

She didn't answer.

"Well?"

"I'm thinking."

"Think quickly because I'm about done."

"Okay. I'll try to go to sleep. Now, tell me what happened."

"Why are you so interested?"

"I think it's because you're the only person I know and I don't even know you. Not really."

He sighed and grumbled something she couldn't make out. "Her name was Eliana. She was Brazilian. We were married for just long enough for her to take me for almost everything I had and get the hell out of town. She wound up back in Brazil, via the rest of South America. It took me six months to track her down."

Good God, no wonder he seemed hard at times. "Did you get your money back?"

"Nope. She'd spent it."

"That's awful. What did you do?"

"Wasn't much I could do except to learn from the experience. I couldn't make her pay what she didn't have.

Besides, it was my fault as much as hers."

"How do you figure that?"

"If I hadn't been so naive and trusting, she'd never have managed to play me like she did."

"Somehow you don't seem like the naive, trusting type."

"I'm not anymore."

"No, you aren't. At least, not with me. You didn't believe me at first. About the amnesia."

"No. You have to admit it's pretty far-fetched."

"I suppose it is." But he had believed her, eventually. "How did you get into your current profession?"

"I used my experience tracking down Eliana to go into the PI business. Specializing in finding missing people. Particularly in South America."

"Is that why you speak Spanish so well?"

"Mostly. I have a good ear for languages."

"Why did you marry her?"

He laughed. "Good question. She was hot and she worked it. Man, did she work it. I was young, stupid, and driven by hormones. Which, come to think of it, is the same thing."

"And you've never trusted a woman since."

She didn't think he was going to answer. Who could blame him? Mitch's feelings about women were none of her business. "I'm sor—"

"No, I haven't."

"That's sad."

"I DIDN'T SAY there'd never been women in my life." Why did it seem important that she know that? Because he'd admitted to being a loser when he was young? And why the hell was he talking to her so frankly? He never talked about Eliana. Never. That had happened years ago. It was just a bad memory and a hard lesson learned.

She laughed. Not just a chuckle but a full-fledged laugh. "Oh, I'm sure there have been."

"What's that supposed to mean?"

"Don't be modest. You have to know women find you attractive."

He barely stopped himself from saying, *Do you?* "Whatever I say you'll either think I'm being overly modest, or conceited as hell. It's a no win."

"You're right. I'm being nosy. Ignore me."

If only he could. "We should get some sleep."

She lapsed into silence. But it didn't last long. "Are you expecting trouble?"

"Always. Why?"

"I just wondered about the gun. You didn't use it earlier when those men tried to abduct me."

"I didn't need to. But it's nice to have it, just in case."

"Do you need it often?"

"Occasionally. I try never to use it, especially down here. I have permits but that doesn't matter a damn if you shoot a local."

"Even a criminal?"

"Yep. Any local."

"So why even have it?"

"If it's a choice between not shooting and saving my ass, or the person I'm protecting, I'm going to save my ass."

"I thought you were a PI. Are you a bodyguard too?"

"I have been at times. I thought we were going to sleep?"

She was quiet, then said in a very small voice, "I can't sleep. I'm worried."

"About what, specifically?"

"Meeting my family I don't remember. Going to the ranch I don't remember. Taking the fake bills to the police. What if they throw me in jail? And you too?"

"Why would they do that?"

"Because they might not believe us. Because...what if they're on the Villareals' payroll?"

"I can see the Argentine police being on their payroll, but it's a little far-fetched to think they'd have Chilean authorities on it."

"It was far-fetched that those men found me in Valparaiso and tried to kidnap me, too. But they did. And they're probably still after me."

Damn, she had a point. "I wouldn't worry about the cops. I have a lot of connections in South America. I have some good contacts with Chilean LEOs. No one is going to throw us in jail."

"We could take everything back to the US."

"No we can't. I'm not smuggling counterfeit bills into the US."

"There must be—"

"Be quiet," Mitch said. Maybe he was paranoid, but that had stood him in good stead before. He rolled out of bed, picked up his gun and stopped by the couch on the way to the door. Leaning down, he whispered in Glenna's ear, "Go into the bathroom. Hide in the tub." He could see her gearing up to argue, even in the darkness of the room. He didn't waste time arguing, but pulled her out of bed by her arm and hustled her into the bathroom.

He stood behind the door to the room, watching as the intruder unlocked the door and then wedged it open in order to hack the door chain. Just as he succeeded, Mitch yanked the door open, grabbed the arm with the gun and took him to the ground. Seconds later, he had him disarmed and face down with his arms behind him. The asshole was so surprised he hadn't said a word. "In case you're curious," he said in Spanish, as the man tried to squirm, "that's a gun I have jabbing into your neck. So if I was you I'd be fucking still." He stopped moving immediately.

"You can come out now," he said to Glenna in English.

She opened the door and peeked out. "Is that—"

"The same guy from this morning? Yeah. Which means his partner is probably around too. Pick up that gun and go look in my bag. I've got some flex-cuffs in the front pocket."

Light spilled out as she came out of the bathroom and

picked up the gun, handling it like she'd done it before. Many times. Not totally surprising since she'd been working on a ranch from the time she was a kid. Still, he'd have thought her more familiar with shotguns than handguns.

"You know handguns," Mitch said as she brought him the cuffs.

"Apparently, I do. It felt comfortable in my hands."

Briefly, he wondered where she'd learned about handguns, but he had to admit he liked seeing her take charge. It gave him a glimpse of her true personality.

The dipshit had recovered enough to threaten and curse him. After Mitch flex-tied his ankles and wrists, he hauled him up. "Shut up."

"*¡Chingate, pendejo!*"

Mitch smacked him and said it again. "*Cállate, boludo.*" He sat him in a chair and asked, "Who sent you?"

"*No lo sé.*" He was a short, wiry man who was completely unremarkable. Other than the fact he stank, but that wasn't too shocking given his profession.

"He says he doesn't know," Mitch said to Glenna. "Too bad. Call the cops."

"*No policía.*"

He continued the conversation in Spanish. "Then talk. Who sent you?"

After a lot of back and forth, it was clear the man didn't know who had hired him and his partner. Or if he did know, he wasn't saying. "This is pointless," Glenna said, and picked up the phone.

"No, no," the man said. "*No policía.*"

"Tell me something useful, then. Why do they want her? What was the plan? What were you supposed to do with her?"

"I don't know. My partner might. We were told to take her to a house in Santiago and await instructions. And bring her belongings with her."

"Address. Give me the address."

He gave it reluctantly and Glenna wrote it down.

"Did you have any more instructions?"

He leered at Glenna. "No. Just to wait until we were contacted. *Pero ella es muy bonita.*"

That simple sentence implied a lot. Mitch looked at Glenna. She looked disgusted. The man was openly grinning now. Deciding to wipe the smile off his ugly face, Mitch punched him in the stomach. While he was gasping Mitch said, "Here's what you're going to do. You're going to call your partner and tell him you need help and he needs to come up here."

"Why should I?" he asked when he'd recovered his breath.

Glenna walked over and casually pointed the gun at him. "Because if you don't I'll shoot you," she said in Spanish. She held the muzzle against his knee. "Right here. I understand being shot in the kneecap is painful. Very painful."

Chapter Ten

H E MUST HAVE believed her, Glenna thought. He told Mitch the number and when Mitch held the phone up to his ear, he asked his partner to help. A short time later, the other kidnapper opened the door, and inside of a minute, Mitch had him disarmed and on the ground, flex-tying his hands and feet.

"You're awfully good at that," Glenna said.

"Practice. I've done it a time or two."

More than that, I bet.

Mitch asked the second kidnapper the same questions he'd asked the first one, with no better results. After gagging them both with pillowcases, Mitch searched them, took their phones and what money they had and then pulled Glenna aside. In a low voice, in English, he said, "You have a choice. Wait and tell the cops everything. If we do that, God knows how long we'll be stuck in Valparaiso. The other choice is to get dressed, pack up and leave, following our original plan. In that case, these two won't face kidnapping charges because we won't be here to corroborate it."

She thought about it, but not for long. "No, I'd rather go and take care of it there." She followed Mitch's lead and didn't say where they were going, or what they were going to take care of. She wasn't sure how much the men could hear and understand but it was better to take no chances.

"Good. I think that's our best course of action. As for these assholes—" he jerked a thumb toward them "—odds are high that they both have extensive criminal records. I doubt they'll get out of jail anytime soon. Especially since they won't have any money. Anyway, we'll be gone."

She wanted to ask questions but knowing they couldn't talk freely, she held her tongue. Ten minutes later, they left the hotel and stopped by the kidnappers' van so Mitch could search and disable it. The search yielded nothing, which at that point was no surprise.

Not long after that, they were on their way. "What happens when we get to Santiago? Are we going to take the counterfeit money to the police?"

"Yes. We have all day tomorrow—I mean today—and tonight to wait until our plane leaves. I want to put distance between us and get rid of this car just in case they manage to talk themselves out of jail."

"Do you think they will?"

"No, but it doesn't hurt to be prepared. It's why I took their cash, their phones and disabled the van." He shot a sharp glance at her. "Are you all right?"

Feeling a little hysterical, she laughed. "No. Not at all."

"I can't blame you. It's a lot to take in." He paused and added, "You're not going to cry, are you?"

She smiled at the wary note in his voice. "Not at the moment. I think I'm cried out. But I'll let you know if I change my mind." She looked out the window but it was dark and she couldn't really see anything. "I'll feel better once all the counterfeit money is out of my hands."

"We'll go to the station first thing. I've got some law enforcement contacts in Santiago."

"You have a lot of contacts everywhere."

"I've spent a good deal of time down here."

"Don't you have some contacts in Valparaiso? Maybe we should have stayed there after all."

"I would have if we didn't have time constraints. Plus we can't be sure how much the Villareals—if it is them—know about your whereabouts. Better to disappear, I think."

"What about the car? Can they trace it?"

"Possibly. But we're going to switch cars with a friend of mine in a little town on the way to Santiago. He'll take our car back to the rental place and pick up his at the airport after we've left the country."

"You said *if* it is the Villareals. I thought you were sure that's who is after me."

"It's the most likely scenario. Especially considering what you've got on them."

A short time later, they'd switched cars with Mitch's friend and were on their way to Santiago again.

"You did good back there."

For a moment she couldn't think what he was referring to. "I didn't do anything except pick up the gun and threaten to kneecap him. I was tempted to do it anyway after hearing him say—imply—they were planning to rape me." She shot a glance at his grim profile. "Thank you for punching him."

"You're welcome. If we'd had time, I'd have done more."

"He seemed surprised when you punched him."

Mitch shook his head. "The guy is as dumb as a box of rocks. His partner's no better." He shot her a glance. "Try to get some sleep. It's going to be at least another hour until we get there."

"What about you?"

"Sleeping while driving's not a good idea."

"Ha, ha. I meant do you need me to stay awake and talk to you so you don't fall asleep?"

"No, I'm good."

She wadded up her coat, placed it against the window, and laid her head on it. Glenna didn't think there was a chance in hell she'd sleep but she closed her eyes anyway. And slept.

"You have to go."

"Not without you."

"I can't. I can't leave Bartolo and he will never go."

"But if you stay—"

"I love him," she said, "whatever he's done. And Bartolo loves me. I'll be all right. But you, you must leave, Glenna.

Before the Señor realizes you are carrying his child."

Valencia was right, but still Glenna hesitated. "I'm afraid for you. If he finds out you helped me he'll kill you."

"He won't find out."

He was heir to an empire. Autocratic, cruel and possessive. His charm, that charm that had so seduced her, was a façade. If she stayed she condemned her child as well as herself to be under his rule, powerless, with no way out.

MITCH DECIDED TO get a room at the large hotel across the street from the airport and try to get some rest before tackling everything they had to do. Since they'd need a room anyway for the night, until their plane left the next day, there wasn't any reason to wait. He could function on no sleep but he preferred having at least a couple of hours of shut-eye.

He would call his friend, Felix, later in the morning after he'd had some sleep. Felix Vasquez was a cop Mitch had known since he'd first come to South America looking for Eliana. Mitch had been back many times over the years. They'd become good friends. Mitch thought Felix would be more sympathetic to their time constraints, and he trusted him absolutely to look into what the Villareals were up to after he and Glenna had left the country.

If he could talk Felix into coming to them, so much the better. For all he knew the Villareals had decided to prosecute Glenna with some kind of trumped-up evidence. Depending on whose palms her former employers had greased, the Chilean police could very well send her back to Argentina.

Which was not going to happen on his watch. He pulled under the porte-cochère and looked at Glenna. She was sound asleep, with her head on her coat, leaning against the window. She looked young and vulnerable, her face pale, her freckles standing out in stark relief. He knew she was thirty, but right now she looked about eighteen. Twenty at the outside. As he watched she moaned and said, "No. No, you can't."

Mitch reached over and touched her arm. "Glenna, wake up." No response. He shook her arm gently and said her name a little louder. She opened her eyes, looking totally at sea. "We're at the hotel."

"Hotel? What—Who—" She sat up with a jerk. "Oh. Mitch. I was dreaming."

"You seemed upset. Did you remember something?"

"It's all mixed up. I was talking to my friend, Valencia. I think she lived on the ranch. She wanted me to leave, to run away. We were both afraid…of him."

"Who?"

She shook her head. "I don't know. I never saw his face or thought his name. But I was afraid for myself, and my baby."

"You're starting to remember. That's good." She didn't look like she agreed with that. "Anything more?"

"No, just impressions. Fear, mostly. And…anger."

"It's a start."

She rubbed her eyes. "Not much of one."

True, but at least it was something. He changed the subject. "It's still really early so I figured we'd get some sleep before I call Felix."

"Who's Felix?"

"My friend who's a Santiago cop. Come on, let's go in. Put your scarf on."

"Do you really think that's necessary?"

He looked at her hair, a long, lush dark red that would draw notice even in a country filled with redheads. Which Chile wasn't. "Yes. Put it on."

"I should have just kept it brown," she grumbled.

"Once you get on the plane it won't matter."

He signed them in as Mr. and Mrs. Garcia. Since they both spoke Spanish like natives it seemed prudent. Glenna took the couch and he took the bed and both of them passed out fully clothed.

Mitch had a fleeting thought just before falling asleep. *What would it be like if Glenna wasn't a job and, therefore, wasn't off limits?*

Which undoubtedly explained why he dreamed about her.

Chapter Eleven

MITCH'S COP FRIEND, Felix Vasquez, was, in a word, gorgeous. Tall, with dark curly hair and dark brown eyes, a blinding smile, and movie star good looks. Glenna did a double take when she met him. *This guy is a cop? In Chile?* When she found out he was a proud father and family man, she was even more surprised.

He was very charming after Mitch introduced them, but the "cop" expression in his eyes, as well as the way he shook her hand and held it a moment, said he was sizing up everything about her. She decided right then and there to let Mitch do the talking and only speak when directly spoken to.

Have I been in trouble with the law before? Or is being familiar with the "cop" stare just from her recent experiences? In the last few weeks she'd spent a lot of time avoiding the cops. Knowing she was hunted but not knowing who was hunting her made her leery of everyone, cops included.

Mitch told his friend the entire story, not leaving anything out. Which obviously meant he trusted this man completely. She wondered what they'd been through together to make Mitch trust him utterly, when it was clear Mitch was not normally the trusting type. She'd known that even before he told her the story about his deceitful ex-wife.

"She really has amnesia?" Felix asked when Mitch stopped, shooting her a skeptical glance.

"I know how it sounds, but yes, she does. She might remember bits and pieces, though we can't be sure of that. Basically, she can't remember a damn thing before waking up in the hospital after the bus accident. I'm convinced it's for real and so are her brothers. We video chatted with them last night."

Some kind of unspoken conversation passed between them. "*¿Es verdad?*" Felix asked finally.

"*Sí, es verdad.*"

Apparently satisfied, Felix nodded. "That's some story. The Villareals. I wonder if they're related to the Peruvian Villareals?"

"Who are they?"

"One of the top counterfeiting crime families in Peru," Felix said dryly. "I'll look into it, but if these Argentine Villareals are counterfeiting then I'm betting the two families are related. That makes me wonder, though, if they'd bring the cops into it if they are running a counterfeiting operation."

"I wondered too, but the local cops could be on their payroll."

"True," Felix agreed. "That's certainly a possibility." He got up to leave saying, "I'll call you later. You should probably lay low until I find out if Glenna's got a warrant out for her arrest in Argentina and whether we've been apprised of it. When are you leaving?"

"Our plane leaves early in the morning. Tell Lila and the kids hi for me."

"Will do. Next time you need to come over for a meal. Lila's going to be pissed she missed out on seeing you." He shook Mitch's hand, nodded at Glenna and left.

"Looks like it will be room service," Mitch said, picking up the menu and handing it to her.

They both ordered sandwiches, which arrived quickly. Glenna waited until they'd both eaten before she broached the subject that she'd been wondering about almost since Mitch had convinced her of her true identity.

She wiped her mouth and hands with a napkin, set it down on the rolling table and said, "Tell me about myself."

"YOU HAVE NO idea how weird that sounds," Mitch said.

"I'm sure it does, but I don't care. Tell me."

"You should talk to your family. They know a lot more than I do, obviously."

"They don't feel like my family. I don't remember anything about them. I want to hear it from you."

He rubbed his hands over his face. Dylan had filled him

in on the part of Glenna's history that seemed important, but it wasn't by any means the whole story. She was depending on him. More and more the longer they were together. He knew why. Hell, she didn't know another soul in the world. He'd found her, convinced her of her real identity, and saved her from being kidnapped. Not to mention, he hadn't hit on her, either. Why wouldn't she depend on him? It should have made him want to head for the nearest exit, yet it didn't.

"Your name is Glenna Leigh Gallagher. You're thirty years old. You have four brothers and you're the next to youngest child."

"I know all that. Tell me things I don't know. Why did I leave home? When did I leave home? How did I come to be working in Argentina? What about my parents? Are they alive or dead?"

He took the last question first. "Your mother died when you were seven or eight. I got the impression you and Dylan, the youngest, were close. I think you mothered him after your mother died. Your father died a few years ago. You came in for the funeral and left within the day. No one knows why. Even though you said you had to get back for work, they suspect it had something to do with your father's will."

"Why?"

"You always wanted to be a rancher, according to Dylan. Your father didn't believe women were suited for that kind of work. You left home at eighteen, after a big fight with your father."

"What was the fight about?"

"Your brothers don't know for sure but they believe your father told you about his will. He split everything equally between all his children, but your inheritance is held in trust until you either turn thirty or get married. If you marry by the time you're thirty, you get your portion. If you don't, it goes to your brothers." He paused and added, "You could still marry and get your inheritance. If you do it before your next birthday." Of course, they couldn't be positive she wasn't married already. To the father of the baby she'd lost.

"That's... That's... Oh, my God. That's the stupidest, most chauvinistic, Neanderthal thing I've ever heard. No wonder I left."

"Yeah, once your brothers found out about that, they weren't surprised you left. They said it was just like you to head off to a completely different country to prove him wrong. The next they heard from you, you were working on a ranch in Argentina. Not the Villareals, but another. Some time before your father died you went to the Villareals' ranch and worked your way up to managing it. Putting you in the perfect position to embezzle, according to the Villareals."

"But they—the Gallaghers—don't believe I embezzled."

"No, and neither do I, for all the reasons we discussed." He added, "I got the impression you were a hellion when you were young. But being a hellion and being dishonest are two different things."

"Only when I was young?"

He smiled slightly. "I don't think they know much about your life since you left home. You kept in touch sporadically until a few months ago. Dylan tried to get in touch with you to ask if you planned to come back for your newest nephew's birth. Your oldest brother Jack married again and their baby was due around Christmas. That's when Dylan found out you'd disappeared from the ranch. Not long after that they hired me to find you."

"How did you get involved?"

"Remember I told you my brother, Austin, is a neurologist in Marietta? He heard they were looking to hire a private investigator who knew South America and suggested me."

"It took you a long time to find me."

Feeling defensive because she was right, he said, "You're very good at losing people. You not only managed to stay hidden from me, you evaded the others who were after you as well. You're extremely resourceful."

His cell phone rang and he answered gratefully. "Hardeman."

"Here's what I found out so far," Felix said. "No embezzlement charges have been filed. However, Rolando Villareal has filed a missing person's report. On his wife."

"Shit."

"I've got worse news. He's planning to charge you with kidnapping."

"That's rich, considering I'm the one who stopped her from being kidnapped. Twice. Why me?"

"Because they knew you were looking for her. And they must know, via the failed kidnapping attempts, that you've found her now."

"You said planning to. Even if he does try to charge me, all Glenna has to do is deny I've coerced her."

"Yes, but I still think you'd better get out of the country as quickly as you can."

"Tomorrow morning, on a nine a.m. flight."

"All right. Be careful, buddy. And don't go anywhere, just to be safe. Neither one of you needs to be seen."

What the hell are we supposed to do between now and tonight, stuck in the room?

I can think of a lot of things.

Things that can't happen. Damn it.

Chapter Twelve

"THAT WAS FELIX, wasn't it?"

"Yes." He was standing with his back to her but he turned around at her question. Still, he said nothing else.

She felt a spurt of annoyance at his silence. Was she going to have to drag everything out of him? "What did he say? It didn't sound good from your side. What was all that about you being charged?"

"Sit down and I'll tell you," he said.

Grudgingly, she sat on the couch and waited for him to continue.

"You're not being charged with embezzlement. Which is good, considering if you were you could be extradited to face the charges."

"Oh, yay," she said sarcastically. "What else?"

"Rolando Villareal claims you two are married."

"What? Married? That means—he must be the one in my dream. But we weren't married." *In her dream. Who knew if that was true?*

"But you don't know," he reminded her. "Unless you've

remembered something and haven't told me."

"No, just what I dreamed. Surely I'd remember something like being married."

"Why? You can't remember you were pregnant. You haven't remembered your brothers, either."

True. Damn it. "He could be lying. Why didn't he tell my brothers we were married when they called, if that's true?"

"I don't know. There are definitely holes in the story. Rolando recently filed a missing persons report on you. Why he waited so long is unclear. But now, according to Felix, he's planning to have me charged with kidnapping."

"You didn't kidnap me. So he can't. Can he?"

"I'm not sure. Neither is Felix. Probably not, if you deny I kidnapped you or coerced you in any way."

"You're still worried."

He rubbed the back of his neck and paced away a few steps. "Yeah, I am. I don't trust the Villareals. I think they'll do whatever it takes to destroy any evidence of their crime."

"But I've turned everything over to the police. It doesn't matter now."

"They don't know that. And if those fake bills make it to an uncorrupted law enforcement agency in Argentina, their operation is toast."

"That's not all, though, is it? Are you afraid they're still going to come after me?"

"It's sure as hell a possibility. Especially since they probably still believe you've got evidence on their operation. Regardless, we're leaving the country tomorrow morning. But in the meantime, we have to stay here."

"Here? You mean here, as in we're stuck in the room? We can't even go to the hotel restaurant?"

"Felix thinks we should stay out of sight until we leave for the airport in the morning."

"Great. What are we going to do for the next nine or ten hours until it's time to go to bed?"

Mitch had a funny look on his face. But he only said, "Surf the web, watch TV. Sleep."

"If I sleep now I won't sleep tonight."

He shrugged. "Watch TV. Or you can use my computer. Look up Marietta and your family. Look up the Villareal ranch. Look up the Villareals. Maybe something will spark a memory."

"If I'm using your computer what are you going to do?"

"I'm going to sleep. I can pretty much sleep anywhere, anytime."

Glenna spent the next few hours watching TV and surfing the web on Mitch's computer. She looked up everything she could find about Marietta, the Gallaghers and the Villareals, but nothing created a spark of remembrance. Well, that wasn't totally correct. When she'd seen a picture of Rolando Villareal she'd gotten a bad feeling, but that could have been due to the dream. She was almost certain now that the man in her dream, the one she was running away from, was Rolando.

True to his word, Mitch stretched out on top of the bed-spread and was asleep within minutes. From time to time she looked over at him. He really was a good-looking guy. She'd noticed it before, the first time she'd seen him. After all, she didn't see men like him or his buddy Felix, for that matter, every day. But she hadn't had a chance to study him like she could now that he was asleep. His dark brown hair was wavy and almost reached his collar, mostly one length with medium sideburns. His face was stubbled, whether by design or simply because he hadn't had time to shave, she didn't know. He had a straight nose, well-defined eyebrows and unusually pretty eyes that changed color easily.

He didn't look young or innocent sleeping. In sleep he looked much as he did awake: a strong, capable man who could handle himself in a variety of situations. His gun and back holster lay on the nightstand beside him. She bet if she yelled or he heard a strange sound, he'd wake up instantly and have the gun in hand in seconds.

Far from bothering her, she liked knowing that. It made her feel safe. Which, with the Villareals and their hirelings looking for her, was important. Though she was tempted to test her theory, she didn't. First of all, he looked peaceful and she knew he had to be tired still. Second, because she had a feeling it would really piss him off.

It was hard to know for sure, of course, but Glenna wanted to believe she was normally a confident, accomplished woman. But if she was so accomplished then why had the cattle business she'd been managing been run into the ground? Why had the Villareals lost their money? Because of something Glenna did or didn't do? She had no idea. Mitch and her family were giving her the benefit of the doubt. Glenna wasn't so sure she deserved it. Even if she had screwed up, though, that didn't mean the Villareals' descent into crime could be pinned on her.

Putting that possibility aside, she thought about Mitch, a much more pleasant topic. She was getting to know Mitch. She liked him. To be honest, she more than liked him. The man was hot. And yeah, he was the only man she knew. Whatever. It didn't matter, both because she had no idea if she was married or whether that was a lie, and because she suspected Mitch thought of her as just a job, and a pain in the ass at that. She went back to the Internet with a sigh.

A few minutes later Mitch woke up. "Find anything helpful?" he asked, still lying on the bed.

"Nothing that jarred my memory. Is there a way to find out if I'm really married?"

"I can have my assistant look into it if you want."

"I need to know. I haven't read anything about Rolando Villareal getting married on the Internet. Which to me is a good indication that he was lying. The Villareal spread and their legitimate business are well known. I'd think there would have been something about the wedding in the society pages, at the least. Even if not, it should be possible to find some record of it."

He got up and walked over to the desk to look over her shoulder at the computer. "Pictures didn't help, huh?"

"No." Maybe she wasn't going to remember. Ever. "I looked up Marietta too. Same result. I did like the pictures of the ranch, and particularly Dylan's horses, but I don't know if that means anything."

"Let me look at a site I know. I might find the answer to your question there." He reached over to type on the keyboard.

"Do you want me to move?"

He turned his head to look at her and their eyes met. They locked gazes for a long, long moment. His eyes were gray-blue now, dark-lashed and beautiful. His mouth was close, and very tempting.

His gaze fastened on her lips. Flicked back to her eyes, and then to her mouth again. If he kissed her would his kiss be gentle or rough? Leisurely or urgent? What if she kissed him? Would he pull back? Or move closer?

They both looked away.

What the hell is the matter with me? I shouldn't be thinking about kissing him.

"What did you say?"

"I asked if you wanted me to move. So you could get to the keyboard more easily."

"No, you're fine." He went back to typing so quickly she wondered if she'd imagined that momentary reaction.

She didn't think so.

He pulled up a site, then typed in a query. "There's nothing here, right off," he said after a quick look. "Louise will look into it more thoroughly. I'll email her the details."

Glenna pushed the chair back and stood. "Here, sit down."

He took her place and she wandered over to the window. The view overlooked the airport entrance, but behind that you could see the Andes. Beautiful mountains that gave her a feeling of familiarity. Could that be because Marietta sat between two mountain ranges? Or did it simply mean she'd seen the Andes before?

A little while later Mitch pushed himself away from the desk and said, "I sent Louise the information. She'll get back to me as soon as she finds something. Or if she doesn't. I'm good online but Louise is amazing. If there's something to find, she'll find it."

Glenna nodded, then said, "This is off the subject, but I've been wondering something."

"About what?" He sounded wary.

"That thing you did when those men tried to break into the hotel room. When you took their guns."

"Yeah, what about it?"

"Can you teach me how to do it?"

"Teach you how to disarm someone with a gun?"

"Yes. What if it happens again and you're not around?"

"One reason we're stuck in the room is so it won't happen again. But—" he added before she could protest, "it sure as hell won't hurt you to know how to react if someone pulls a gun on you. It's not like no one ever gets mugged."

"So you'll do it?"

"Sure. Why the hell not?" He walked to the bedside table, picked up his gun and took out the magazine, then emptied the chamber. "Okay, the first thing is you need to remain calm. Which sounds stupid, I know. But when you panic, you freeze and that can be deadly."

Then he took her through two different scenarios: one when the gunman was behind her and one where he was facing her. He didn't simply show her how, he made her practice over and over until he was satisfied she'd learned the lesson. Or at least she'd thought he was satisfied until he said, "Now, practice this daily until it becomes second nature."

"Daily? Are you kidding?"

"Hell, no, I'm not kidding. If you're serious about learning to disarm someone, you need to practice. A lot."

And who am I supposed to practice with when you're gone? But she didn't say it aloud because she didn't want to think about Mitch leaving. Not until she had to.

"It's not time for dinner yet," Glenna said. "I've got a deck of cards in my backpack. We could play card games."

"You remember how to play card games?"

"I do." It was one way she'd made enough money to support herself while she'd been on the run.

His eyes narrowed. "Why do I think there's more to it?"

She hid a grin. "I can't imagine. How about a little poker?"

"Poker, huh." He studied her and said, "You're a card shark."

"I WOULDN'T CALL myself a card shark."

"Which means you are."

"Surely you're not afraid to play me."

"Deal 'em." He took a seat at the table and watched her shuffle and deal. She handled the cards with great familiarity. After the first hand, he was certain. Yep, she was a shark all right.

"I'm glad we weren't playing for real money," Mitch said an hour later. "Damn, you're good."

"Thanks. I wonder where I learned how to play like that?"

"Like a killer shark, you mean?"

"You flatter me. I'm not *that* good." She sighed and scooped up her pile of "winnings". Mostly pieces of paper with amounts written on them, but there were a few coins too. "When I couldn't find work I played poker. Most men down here don't think a woman can play that well, so it was usually easy to make enough to tide me over until the next town and the next job."

"You didn't have problems finding games?"

"No, the men were anxious to play with me because they thought I'd be easy pickings. And it's not like I played professional poker."

It would have been funny to see the men's reactions once they found out how wrong they'd been. "You do have four brothers. I suspect they taught you."

Shrugging, she said, "I guess." She folded her hands together on top of the table. "Do you think I'm ever going to remember?"

"Everything?"

"Anything."

She sounded so forlorn. Mitch tried to imagine what it would feel like to suddenly be adrift in the world, not knowing a soul. To have to fend for yourself in that situation, not to mention, running from a threat you couldn't even be sure was real. And then have the threat turn out to be all too real.

He reached over, covered her hand with his and patted it. "I'm sure you'll remember something. Total amnesia is rare, I believe." Honestly, he wasn't at all sure of that, but he didn't think it would hurt her to retain some hope. She didn't speak. He squeezed her hand lightly. "Hey, you're doing a hell of a lot better than I would be in your place. Better than ninety-nine percent of people would be, I'm sure." It would be way too easy to fall under the spell of her green eyes, so full of trust, trust in him. He let go of her hand and stood up. "Are you hungry? We could order dinner."

"I'm not that hungry but if you want something we can go ahead and order."

He picked up the menu. "I'm going to have a steak sandwich. What do you want?"

"A steak sandwich is fine." She got up from the table and walked over to him.

Just as he was about to pick up the phone, she spoke. "Mitch, can I ask you something?"

"Sure."

"You're going to think it's strange."

"Does it have to do with food?"

"No."

"Okay, I'll bite. What is it?"

"Would you mind…holding me?"

For a minute he just stared at her. "Hold you?" His voice damn near cracked.

"I'm not trying to hit on you, I swear. But I just need some human contact. So would you mind?"

Mind? Hell, no, he didn't mind. But he knew it would be a mistake. What was he supposed to say? No? No, because I want to do more than that? Way more than just hold you? He could either refuse, in which case he'd feel like a real dick or he could suck it up and do what she asked. And hope that he could keep his shit together long enough to simply hold her and not do something totally off limits. Like kiss her. And strip off her clothes and make love to her. *Don't even go there.*

"Never mind. Forget I asked. It was stupid."

"Come here," he said gruffly and held out his arms. She walked into them like she belonged there. She wrapped her arms around his waist and laid her head against his chest. He put his arms around her and simply held her, doing his damnedest to think of something, anything else other than that he held a beautiful woman in his arms and he couldn't even kiss her.

Or could he?

No, you dumbshit, you can't.

They stood there a while, in each other's arms, without speaking. "What are you thinking?" she asked.

"You don't want to know." Well, fuck, how did that slip out? What better way to make a woman curious?

"I think I do."

He put his hands on her shoulders and stepped away from her, but he couldn't make himself let go. Searching her eyes, he saw guileless trust in hers. *Of course she's guileless. How could she lie? She didn't know enough about herself to lie.*

There was something else in her eyes, damn it. Desire. And no, he wasn't imagining it. Her lips were full and tempting, and for a moment he wished he had no scruples. But, damn it, he did. His fingers tightened on her shoulders before he released her, turned away and said harshly, "This is not going to happen."

She didn't pretend ignorance. "Why?"

"Do I really have to list the reasons?"

"It's just a kiss, Mitch."

Apparently, he did. "A kiss that isn't going to happen. You're a client. I don't kiss my clients."

"My brothers are your clients, not me."

"A technicality. You have amnesia. That should be reason enough."

Her brows knit together. "I don't see why. I have amnesia, therefore you can't kiss me?"

He ground his teeth before answering. "You don't know who you are. You could be married. Or in love with someone. Not an unreasonable possibility, considering you were pregnant."

"If I am married, and I don't believe I am, then my husband is a criminal who I was so afraid of that I ran away regardless of the fact I was carrying his child."

"Maybe the baby wasn't his. Maybe you're in love with someone else," he said a little desperately. "The father of your baby."

"You're really grasping at straws, aren't you? I think the fact that I was on the run proves that whoever the father was, I didn't want any part of him."

"Maybe."

"What are you so afraid of? Or are you not attracted to me and you're having a hard time telling me that?"

He let out a sharp laugh. "Yeah, I wish that was the problem." He looked at her and shook his head. "Stop

RETURN OF THE COWGIRL

looking at me like that. You're a beautiful woman and I'm a single man who hasn't been with a woman in way too long."

She was full-out smiling now.

"Damn it, Glenna, we're all alone here. The room is soundproof. I could do anything I wanted to you and you couldn't do a damn thing about it."

"Oh, yes, I could." She walked to the nightstand and picked up his gun. "I could shoot you."

"You could try. But you might miss. I taught you how to disarm a gunman. Do you really think I couldn't disarm you?"

"This is stupid, Mitch," she said, laying down the gun. "You're not going to do anything I don't want you to do, and I'm not going to shoot you."

This was getting way out of hand. He decided the only way to deal with it was to ignore it. "I'm going to order dinner."

"Chicken."

He picked up the receiver and looked at her. "Damn straight."

Chapter Thirteen

L AST NIGHT IT had taken Glenna a long time to fall asleep. She spent a while thinking about what had passed between her and Mitch. And what hadn't happened.

That went well, Ms. Realist said.

Hey, he admitted he was attracted to me, Ms. Ever-hopeful answered.

Sort of. It wasn't much of an admission. What do you think you're doing?

If you must know, I wondered if kissing Mitch might bring back some memories. Like of the father of my baby. You know, the baby I can't remember either?

Oh, bullshit. You want to kiss him because you think he's hot. It has nothing to do with getting your memory back.

Not true. Or not totally. I like him. He's an interesting guy. I feel like I know him, which at this point is a huge plus. Besides, Mitch makes me feel safe. And right now I find that extremely attractive.

Was it any wonder she dreamed about him when she finally fell asleep?

And now it was morning. Time to get out of South

RETURN OF THE COWGIRL

America and into the US. To see her family, a family she didn't know from a hole in the ground.

"How long is our flight?" Glenna asked Mitch, pouring herself another cup of coffee from the breakfast tray he'd ordered.

"The one to Houston is about ten hours. Then we have a layover overnight. There aren't any flights to Bozeman until the next day."

"So we'll be traveling for two days."

"You got it."

She'd have some time in the US before getting to Montana. More time with Mitch. Would he leave Marietta as soon as he dropped her off? Or would he stick around for a while? Maybe he would, since his brother lived there.

Glenna was jumpy, half expecting someone to snatch her walking into the airport or even at the gate. But they made it on board without any problems.

The flight was long and boring. Even though Glenna had bought a book at the airport gift store, she couldn't get into it. Mitch ignored her, or tried to. She caught him watching her several times during the flight, when she'd thought he was asleep, but he never said much. Mostly, he slept. Or pretended to.

Glenna tried to sleep but couldn't. She tried several more times to read but the book she'd picked up—without reading the description—was about an abused woman running for her life. That hit too close to home, even though she didn't actually know what had happened to her.

Even so, she knew she'd been on the run at least since leaving the hospital. According to Mitch, for longer than that. Running, so Mitch thought, from the Villareals. She searched her mind for any memories of the Villareals or the ranch she'd lived on for a number of years. Bits and pieces. Fragments of dreams, scenes she couldn't be sure were true or imagined.

What was Rolando Villareal like—besides being a criminal? What made her leave the ranch? Finding out the Villareals were running a counterfeiting operation or was it something else? Something worse?

"Mitch, wake up." She shook his arm.

"What?" He came awake instantly, sat up and looked around. "We aren't there yet, are we?"

"No, we still have hours. Have you heard anything from Felix?"

He looked annoyed as he settled back in his seat. "You woke me up to ask that? No. For one thing, I'm not paying for an Internet connection when we'll have one free tonight. For another, Felix only heard our story yesterday. He needs to verify that the money is counterfeit and he needs time to contact the proper authorities if it is."

"What if nothing comes of it? What if the Argentinian authorities blow him off? What if they're on the Villareal's payroll?"

"Every law enforcement agency in Argentina can't be on

102

their payroll. Stop worrying. It's out of our hands. Felix will handle it. You've done what you can and now you need to concentrate on getting your memory back and being with your family. Let the rest of it go."

THEY CHECKED INTO separate rooms at the hotel. She shouldn't need a bodyguard in the States. One more night and another plane ride and he could turn Glenna over to her family. The thought should have been a relief.

It wasn't.

He should have been happy that the job was nearly done. He wasn't.

He could go back to Texas, leaving any further investigation of Glenna's case to his assistant, and take another job. A job that could lead him anywhere. Like back to South America, or anywhere else in the world. That's what he did. He liked moving around. Staying in one place for too long didn't suit him.

Still, he could afford to take some time off to visit Austin. He hadn't seen his brother in months. Austin was always after him to come to Marietta and stay awhile. Here was the perfect opportunity.

Of course it had nothing to do with Glenna Gallagher. Glenna, who he wouldn't be responsible for much longer. Glenna, who he'd wanted to kiss almost from the first time he saw her, sitting alone in the café in Chile. Glenna, who would have kissed him last night if he could have left his scruples behind.

She should be able to make her own decisions. Damn it, she was a grown woman.

A grown woman with amnesia, bozo.

He heard a knock and then Glenna's voice, asking, "Are you ready to get some dinner?"

He opened the door and did a double take. Upon arriving at the hotel, she'd "borrowed" some money and gone to the gift shop. As a result, she wore a shirt he'd never seen and for the first time since he'd known her, she wore makeup. Her eyes looked enormous, with long black lashes and the color a deep emerald green. Her lips were fire-engine red, slick and inviting. She wore a simple, white, button-down blouse that on her looked anything but simple. Her jeans were the same ones she'd been wearing, tight enough to be very distracting when they weren't paired with an oversized, long top.

And her hair. *Jesus help me, her hair.* It had obviously just been washed. It gleamed dark red, full, curling and spilling over her shoulders and down her back. He wanted to sink his hands in her hair, tilt her head back, and ravage her with his mouth. And his hands. And any part of his body he could rub against her.

"Mitch? Why are you staring at me?"

My God, he was nearly struck dumb. "I'm not," he gritted out. He stepped out into the hallway and shut the door behind him.

It was going to be a long night. At least they were eating at the hotel, so the meal probably wouldn't take long.

Wrong again. The service was excruciatingly slow.

"Do you suppose the waitress forgot to put in our order?" Glenna said after half an hour.

"I hadn't thought of that. Maybe she did." He flagged her down. "Do you know how much longer our food is going to be?"

"I'll go check."

"While you're back there bring us some bread."

"That will cost extra."

He barely stopped himself from saying, "I don't give a flying shit what it costs, just bring us some food." But he managed to control himself. "Fine. Just bring us the bread, and soon."

After she left, Glenna shot him a mischievous glance. "I thought you were going to explode when she said it would cost extra."

"I'm surprised I didn't." His mood had nothing to do with hunger—not hunger that could be cured with food, anyway. The waitress brought out the bread, assured them that their meal would be there soon and left.

Mitch picked up a piece of bread, slapped some butter on it and stuffed some in his mouth. "She said soon at least forty-five minutes ago," he grumbled after he swallowed.

Glenna helped herself to a piece of bread. "Too bad neither of us is drinking. I know why I'm not but why don't you? Because you're on the job? You're not still worried about someone following us, are you?"

"No." Although there was nothing to stop the Villareals from hiring someone in the States to come for Glenna. They would almost certainly know she would be going to Montana, though they couldn't be sure where they came into the US. "Not yet, anyway."

"Meaning you think they'll keep looking for me?"

"No way of knowing. But you'll be fine at your family ranch. Marietta is a small town and strangers stick out."

"That's comforting. I guess." She ate another piece of bread. "You never did say why you don't drink. Am I being too nosy?"

"No, it's not a secret. I limit myself to one drink, and there's a good reason for that."

"What is it?"

"Not it. Her. Eliana."

"Your ex?"

"Yes. We got married in Vegas, during a long, drunken weekend. I was really young and really stupid once. I don't plan to repeat it."

"Do you honestly think you could be taken in again?"

"No, but I'm going to make damn sure I'm not."

She tilted her head and studied him. "I think you're much too cynical to fall for a con again."

"Not cynical. Realistic." Their eyes met and he added, "I

have a weakness for beautiful women."

She laughed. "Well, that lets me out."

"Are you kidding?" She didn't know she was beautiful? "Have you looked in a mirror recently?"

"Yes, right before dinner. I saw a redhead with freckles. Hardly a femme fatale."

Good God, she was serious. He shook his head. He knew they were getting into dangerous territory but he couldn't leave it alone. "I don't know how to break it to you, Glenna, but you're one of the most beautiful women I've ever met."

She stared at him. "Wh—Wh—What did you say?"

"Here's your dinner," the waitress said, plopping their dishes down in front of them. "Sorry it took so long."

Glenna sat unmoving, staring at him.

"Eat your dinner," he said, and applied himself to his.

Chapter Fourteen

*H*OW CAN HE *say something like that and then just calmly eat his dinner?* Clearly, he was finished discussing it. Glenna tried to pretend like it was no big deal but it was. She'd worked hard the last few months to become invisible. And she'd succeeded because no one had given her a second glance. Exactly what she had wanted.

When she'd changed her hair color back to the original red, she'd thought she looked good. Or at least better.

But it was an undeniable shock to discover that Mitch thought she was beautiful.

Neither of them said much through the rest of dinner. She had no clue what Mitch was thinking about but she was wrestling with her feelings about him. Obviously, she was crushing on him. Because he was protective, understanding, and totally, seriously hot? Or simply because he was the only man she knew? How was she supposed to know the answer to that?

Their rooms were on the same floor, a couple of doors down from each other. Mitch walked her to her door and waited while she got out her key card and opened it. "To-morrow's the day," she said.

"You look like you're nervous."

"Of course I am. I'm meeting my 'family'," she said, making air quotes, "for the first time."

"Relax. They're good guys. And they're all married, except Dylan, and he's engaged. You'll have some women to talk to as well. You won't feel out of place for long."

Sure I won't. And once I see them I'll instantly regain my memory.

Fat chance.

"What if they hate me?"

"Your brothers? Why would they?"

"I don't know. Maybe their wives won't like me."

"Now you're just worrying to be worrying. There's no reason the wives won't like you."

Maybe. "Do you want to come in?" She didn't know why she asked when she knew he wouldn't.

He smiled and shook his head. Then he touched the back of his fingers to her cheek, a gentle brush that nevertheless sent a little thrill up her spine. "Get some sleep."

Sleep. Would she dream of her past? Something important from her past? Or would she dream about Mitch? Her money was on Mitch.

GETTING TO MONTANA was a long, if uneventful trip. They had to stop and change planes twice, which was a pain. But they finally arrived in Bozeman around mid-afternoon. After they landed, Mitch rented a car and they were on their way—all too soon for Glenna's comfort.

"They're your family, not your enemy," Mitch said after they'd been driving a while.

Glenna yanked her gaze away from the Gallatin mountains to the east of them, to look at Mitch. "I know that. Why would you say that?"

"Because you've hardly said a word since we got in the car at the airport and your expression is more suitable for someone facing a firing squad than it is for someone about to see their family."

"That's ridiculous," she snapped, though he had a point. "I'm a little nervous. BFD."

Mitch laughed. "Apparently, it is a big fucking deal. You're more wound up now than you were after the failed kidnapping attempt."

Since that was true, she didn't dispute him. Instead she said, "They may be *seeing* me but I'll be *meeting* them. What if it's all a big mistake and I'm not really her? What if once they see me in person they know I'm a fraud? What do I do then?"

"You are Glenna Gallagher. I'm as sure of that as I am my own name, and I don't have amnesia. How many times do I have to tell you that you are Glenna?"

"A lot." She answered to the name Glenna now. Mitch had been calling her by that name since they met, and by now it didn't sound so strange. But she didn't *feel* like Glenna Gallagher, the long-missing sister. She didn't know who she felt like, only that it wasn't this woman the Gallagher family badly wanted her to be.

Mitch pulled off the road. "We're getting close to the turnoff. Take some time to pull yourself together. Look around. See if any of the scenery rings any bells."

They had been in Paradise Valley for a good while now, heading south on Highway 69. It was beautiful, with the trees and fields turning green in the late spring weather. The horses and cows were out in the fields, along with their offspring. Crops were growing, some just starting, some more established. It was a breathtaking panorama of land, set in between two mountain ranges: the Absaroka to the east and the Gallatins to the west.

And none of it was one bit familiar.

Her distress must have shown on her face because Mitch put his hand on her shoulder with a comforting squeeze. "Don't push it. Your memory will come back when it's ready."

She felt tears prick at her eyes and furiously willed them away. She refused to believe she was a crybaby on top of everything else. "You can't possibly know that."

"Thinking the worst won't get you anything but upset. Will you let me set you up with my brother? I don't know if he can help you, but if he can't he might know someone who can."

His brother, the neurologist. What the hell. It couldn't hurt. "All right. Thanks."

"Anytime. I wish I could do more."

"You can." She leaned across the console and said, "Kiss me."

"That won't help you remember anything."

"I don't care. That's not why I asked. I don't know how long you're planning to stick around but I don't want you to leave without at least getting to kiss you."

He looked into her eyes for a long moment but didn't speak.

"And don't pretend you don't want to. I may have amnesia but I'm not stupid."

"Hell," he muttered. He put his hands on either side of her face, brought her close and kissed her.

My God, did he kiss her.

His lips were soft, his mouth moved over hers slowly. His tongue slipped inside her mouth, tasting, teasing. Slow. Deliberate. Achingly hot. She tasted him as he tasted her, until her breasts tingled and an ache throbbed between her thighs. He kissed her as if he had all day, as if kissing her was his sole focus. Glenna put her arms around his neck, wishing they weren't in the car so that she could get closer to him.

Finally, Mitch broke the kiss and dropped his hands, moving away from her at the same time.

As first kisses went, it was a doozy. Not that she could remember any other kisses. Still, something told her that kissing Mitch had been anything but ordinary. Glenna put her fingers to her mouth. "Wow."

His mouth curved up in a sexy smile. But his words were anything but. "That was a mistake."

"Why do you say that?"

"For a variety of reasons." He pulled off the shoulder back onto the highway.

"I can't think of any. Name one."

He shot her an annoyed glance. "You could be married."

"We've been through that. If I am married I'm married to a bad guy and I'm getting a divorce. Next."

"You have amnesia."

"Really? I hadn't noticed."

"Very funny. Seriously, Glenna, no matter what I want, it wouldn't be right to take advantage of you."

"What do you want, Mitch?" she asked, ignoring the latter part of his statement.

He didn't say anything but his hands tightened on the wheel. "That's not important."

"It is to me."

Chapter Fifteen

S HIT. TRUST GLENNA to focus on that slip of the tongue. He sensed he was sliding down a slippery slope. *I want you. Under me, on top of me, against the wall, on the floor, in a bed, any damn place I can have you.* But obviously, he couldn't tell her that. He shook his head. "Not going to happen, Glenna."

"What if I never regain my memory? Am I supposed to put my life on hold forever? If that's what you think, forget it. That's bullshit."

"No one said anything about forever. And you're not putting your life on hold. You're going to meet your family and once you do—"

"Once I do my memory will come rushing back and everything will be wonderful?"

"It could happen." Jesus, did he sound as desperate as he felt?

"It could," she agreed. "And a meteorite could hit us at this exact moment. That doesn't mean either of those things is going to happen. Or is even likely to happen."

He started to answer but his cell phone rang. Saved by the proverbial bell. He'd left his phone in the cup holder since the car's hands-free device had been disabled. "Can you get that and hand it to me?"

"Mitch's phone," she answered after picking it up. "Just a minute."

"It's Louise. She says she's your assistant."

"She is. Thanks." He took the phone and asked, "What have you found out?"

"I can't find any record of a marriage between Rolando Villareal, or for that matter, any Villareal and Glenna Gallagher. I couldn't find a Glenna Gallagher mentioned in a marriage to anyone in Argentina."

"Okay, thanks." He put the phone back and said, "Congratulations. Odds are you aren't married."

"Good. I hated to think I'd have committed myself to a criminal. Of course, if I am married, I'd like to think I married him before I knew what he was."

"It's not confirmed, but Louise couldn't find any record of you marrying in Argentina. That leaves out the possibility that you got married somewhere else, though. Or that it's not recorded but it still took place."

She shrugged. "Even so, that takes care of one problem. Mostly. Now how can I convince you that you wouldn't be taking advantage of me if we—" she hesitated, then said, "let things happen naturally and quit fighting our feelings?"

"We're not talking about feelings, here, Glenna."

"No? Then what are we talking about?"

"Sex. We're talking about sex. We have the hots for each other. It's not surprising. We've been with each other constantly for almost three days." There. It was finally out in the open, not that it mattered.

She laughed. "You think proximity is the only reason we *have the hots for each other?*" she said, making air quotes.

How in the hell had he gotten into this? Oh, yeah, he'd kissed her. And everything spiraled from there. Worse, he wanted to do it again. Kiss her, touch her, taste every inch of her body, bury his hands in her hair and make her come, screaming his name. But that was not going to happen.

"Maybe not the only reason, but it's a big part of it."

He shot her a glance and saw her smiling. She obviously wasn't buying his theory. With good reason. He took another turn, this one leading to the Gallaghers' farmhouse. He stopped a ways short of the place so Glenna could get the whole picture. The house was a two-story, white wooden classic farmhouse. It had a huge wraparound porch with a couple of rockers and a porch swing on either side of the front door. Wildflowers bloomed in part of the massive front lawn, while closer to the house, there was a grass lawn and beds of planted flowers.

"It's pretty."

"Yes, it is."

"You've seen it before?" she asked him.

"Just once, when I came here to talk to Dylan and get

the information I needed to start tracking you down." He put the car in gear and started driving to the rear of the house.

"Where are you going? The front door is right there."

No need to ask if she remembered the house. Obviously, she didn't. "Everyone uses the kitchen door around back."

He stopped the car and turned off the engine. Glenna sat, looking around, taking in the surroundings. Dylan Gallagher's horse-breeding operation had gained a good reputation, and was growing accordingly. There was a stable down the hill from the house, with another partially built building nearby that he guessed would become another stable. An old rusted-out pickup sat beside the original barn. There was a horse in the round pen, several horses in a nearby pasture, and a number of dogs milling around the stables. A couple of dogs, both of them mixed breeds of some type, had come up to the car barking, and were now sitting patiently, waiting to greet them when they got out.

The kitchen door opened and Dylan Gallagher stepped out, along with a petite brown-haired sixty-ish woman Mitch knew was the housekeeper, Glory. Glenna sat frozen, with a deer in the headlights expression on her face. Figuring that given the chance she might sit there forever, he went around and opened her door.

He held out his hand. "It's okay, Glenna. Come on, let's go see them."

The look she sent him damn near broke his heart. *Take*

me with you, her eyes pleaded. *Take me away. Don't leave me here.* It about killed him to smile reassuringly at her, knowing that's exactly what he was going to do. But not right this minute.

How she could, in a heartbeat, go from sexy, engaging and completely sure of herself to this vulnerable woman who wasn't even sure of her name was a total mystery to him. And disconcerting as hell.

The dogs had followed him around to the passenger side of the car. When Glenna got out they didn't jump on her, but they nosed her, clearly encouraging her to pet them. She squatted and laughed when they licked her face and some of the tension left her shoulders. After a bit she gave them each a last pat and straightened. Mitch got her backpack out of the back seat and slung it over one shoulder.

Dylan whistled. "Spike, Rosa, that's enough. Come." The two dogs dashed off to Dylan, then took off for the barn after he said something to them.

Glenna squared her shoulders and began walking—or more like slowly dragging herself—toward Dylan.

Well, shit, isn't this awkward as hell, Mitch thought watching the two of them.

THEY'RE JUST PEOPLE, Glenna told herself. *People who love you. There's no need to be nervous.*

Except she was. Because these people loved Glenna Gallagher. And she was someone else. Who, she didn't quite know. But she felt like an imposter.

Dylan was walking to meet them halfway. Glenna clutched Mitch's arm, praying he wouldn't pull away. She glanced up at him. He gave her another reassuring smile. And it did reassure her, a little, though she wasn't sure why.

Everyone stopped a short distance away from the kitchen door. The woman, Glory, Mitch had told her, waited at the door. The housekeeper, who, according to Mitch, was a second mother to the Gallaghers.

A young woman with dark hair and a heart-shaped face popped into her mind, a pretty girl with a musical laugh and flashing brown eyes. As quickly as the memory had come, it was gone. And this was, definitely, a memory. Valencia. Why did Glenna feel a flash of fear and sorrow when she thought of her? Was she alive? Dead? Is that why she couldn't remember? Because she didn't *want* to remember?

But you did remember. You remembered she told you to leave. And you remembered being scared for her.

"Mitch, thanks for bringing Glenna home." Dylan offered his hand and Mitch shook it. Dylan turned to her and said, "It's good to have you home, Glenna."

"Thank you." Two words were all she could manage. She had no idea what to say. She couldn't very well say it's good to be home when she didn't recognize anything about the place. She let go of Mitch's arm and took a step forward, but then she simply stood there.

Dylan didn't seem to notice anything amiss. He gave her

a swift hug and said, "I hope you two are hungry. Glory's been cooking for two days."

"Aren't you a sight for sore eyes," Glory said, stepping forward and enveloping Glenna in an enthusiastic hug. She smelled like cookies. Glenna felt a twinge of something. Not quite memory but, perhaps, familiarity?

Turning to Mitch, Glory added, "Lean down here so I can hug you too. Thank you for bringing our girl back to us."

Mitch laughed and hugged her. "Yes, ma'am. You're welcome."

"Would you like to go to your room and freshen up?" Glory asked Glenna as they all went into the kitchen. "Or would you rather eat something first? Dylan, you bring her bags up to the room."

"I only have this backpack." She took it from Mitch and said, "I can get it." Her backpack was literally held together with duct tape. She hadn't wanted to spend any money on a new one and after they opened hers up to find the money and her passport and DNI card, it was falling apart. She was suddenly aware of how she must look, with her hair curling wildly, wearing her only pair of jeans and a T-shirt she'd bought at a half-price sale in the airport gift shop.

"I'll come with you and make sure you have everything you need," Glory said after exchanging a glance with Dylan.

"Thank you." She meant it. She thought it was very considerate of Glory not to call attention to the fact that she didn't know the way to "her" room.

"Dylan, you give Mitch something to eat. And there's some of that beer you like in the fridge."

Glory led her out of the kitchen and through the living room, a very homey-feeling room with a huge stone fireplace, wood floors scattered with rugs, and a comfortable-looking well-worn leather couch and overstuffed chairs. She stopped, struck by the view from one of the large picture windows on either side of the fireplace.

"Oh, my God, what an amazing view." It was a fairy-tale vista. The well-kept lawn surrounded the house. Farther beyond that lay green fields dotted with horses and cattle, with patches of wildflowers springing up here and there. Behind it all, white-topped mountains rose in shades of purples, blues, and grays, against an achingly bright blue sky, darkening even as she watched.

"You always loved this view of the mountains," Glory said. "Ever since you were a little girl."

"I can see why. It's stunning." But she didn't remember. Not even the smallest memory.

Glenna followed Glory up the stairs, turned left and then halted at the first door on the right. "We still call this Glenna's room but we turned it into a guest room a long time ago. We left a few of your favorite things in here."

She opened the door and Glenna followed her in. The walls were painted a pale mint green. A queen-sized bed in a white wrought-iron frame drew her attention next. The bed was covered with a white comforter with mint and white striped throw pillows and a blanket also in mint green completing it.

A small white writing desk stood beneath a window, which had a view of the front lawn. There was a white dresser with a mirror hanging over it. The mirror was framed in the round and sported Mickey and Minnie Mouse figurines. All the woodwork was painted white. "It's beautiful," she said. She stepped closer to the mirror and picked up a picture of a young girl and her horse. "Is this me?"

"Yes. And Minnie, your favorite horse when you were a girl."

She laughed. "After Minnie Mouse. I guess that explains the mirror."

"Yes, you absolutely loved that mirror. We thought you'd want a more grown-up mirror once you became a teenager, but you never did. So we kept it after you left. This bedroom is usually reserved for women. It's a bit too feminine for the men."

"I think it's lovely," she said, looking around.

"So the backpack is all you have?"

"Yes. I don't have many clothes so I'll need to use the washer and dryer if that's okay."

"Of course it is. You're about Sam's size. I'm sure she has some things she won't mind lending you."

"Sam?"

"Dylan's fiancée."

"Is she living here?"

"Mostly. She's trying to sell her house, so sometimes she stays there. Sam's a doctor at the Marietta hospital, like Jack, Sean, and Wyatt. She's a trauma surgeon."

Crap. A trauma surgeon? That sounded intimidating.

Get a hold of yourself. This isn't like you. You're not a vulnerable wimp.

How do you know?

Good question.

"I'll leave you alone. You come downstairs whenever you're ready."

"Glory? Would you mind staying and talking to me a little?"

"Of course not."

Glenna couldn't get any words out. Staring out the window, she felt her throat close up and tears prick her eyes. *Damn it, I'm not going to cry. There's no reason to. I'm with my family. Yes, and Mitch is leaving soon.* That thought depressed her even more.

"Glenna, honey, don't you worry. This will all come back to you when it's good and ready."

She turned and gazed at Glory, thinking how motherly and comforting she looked. Glory held out her arms. Glenna walked in to them and began crying in earnest. Though Glory was nearly a head shorter than her, it was a relief to feel as if she could lay some of her burden down, if only for a little bit.

"There, there," Glory murmured. "Cry it out, sweetie."

She did for a while, then finally forced herself to stop and move out of Glory's arms. "I don't usually cry like that. Do I?" She wiped her eyes and blew her nose with the tissue Glory handed her.

"You never did as a girl. Well, you cried a time or two when you were hurt. When you tangled with the barbed wire fence, the time you broke your arm, and a few other things."

"Good. I don't want to find out I'm a wimp."

Glory laughed. "Oh, girl, that's the last thing you were. And still aren't, I'll bet the ranch."

"I don't remember anything about the family, or about the ranch either," Glenna said, her breath hitching. "None of it."

"You have amnesia," Glory said reasonably. "Doesn't mean it won't get better. You won't do yourself any good worrying yourself sick about it, so just relax. Your memory will come back when it's good and ready. You were always headstrong. Guess your memory is too."

Glenna smiled. There was something infinitely comforting about Glory. She sat on the bed and Glory took the upholstered chair in the corner.

"When did I leave home?"

"A long time ago. You weren't much older than eighteen."

"Mitch said—He said I had a fight with my father and left home and hardly came back in all the time since."

Glory nodded. "Your daddy—he was a good man. But

he had a blind spot about women and ranching. He just didn't believe a woman should be running a ranch. Since that's what you were determined to do, you two got into it more than once. I don't know exactly what passed between you that time that caused you to up and leave but I do know he regretted it."

"If that's so, why did he cut me out of the will?"

"Oh, honey, he didn't cut you out. Well, not exactly."

"Mitch told me there was something in there about how I wouldn't inherit anything unless I married by the time I was thirty. Or before I turn thirty-one, anyway." Which, according to her passport, was in a couple of months. Not that it mattered. She wasn't going to take anything from the Gallaghers anyway. At least not until her memory came back. If it did.

Shaking off that thought, she changed the subject. "Did I keep in touch with anyone?"

"You wrote to Dylan regularly. You two were close. Closest in age and closest in what you loved."

"What did we love?"

"Horses. Both of you were always horse crazy."

"I haven't been around a horse since… I don't remember the last time." Tomorrow she'd ask Dylan to let her see the horses. Maybe that would help, although she didn't hold out a lot of hope.

"I imagine you were around a lot of horses on that ranch you worked at."

She shrugged. "I don't know. I can't remember that either."

"What do you remember, honey?"

"Almost nothing before the accident. Everything from the time I woke up in the hospital. I've had a few dreams and a few flashbacks. At least, I think that's what they are. They're all about Argentina, though."

"That makes sense. You've been living in Argentina and you haven't lived here in a long time."

"I feel so bad that I can't remember them."

"Your brothers? Don't you worry about them. They're just thrilled to pieces to have you home." She paused and added, "I can't imagine what that must be like. What do the doctors say about you remembering?"

"I haven't seen any since I left the hospital in Chile. Mitch wants me to see his brother. He's a neurologist here in Marietta."

"That sounds like a good idea. You're sweet on Mitch, aren't you?"

Sweet on. What an old-fashioned saying. Glory didn't look all that old. "I—He's the only person I know."

"It'd be a pity if that's all there is to it. He is one fine-looking man. And from what I can tell, he's just fine period."

Glenna couldn't argue with that. "He is. Yes, he is."

Glory said, "I'll leave you to yourself for a bit, but don't forget there's food downstairs. Since we weren't sure when you'd get here I put out sandwich makings. Your other brothers are coming over in a little while. They all want to see you. And they want to talk to Mitch."

"Okay."

"The rest of the family will be over tomorrow for dinner. Although you'll meet Sam today when she gets off work." At the door, she paused and added, "It's a lot of people, so don't feel like you can't go outside or down to the stables or up to your room, or wherever if it gets to be too much for you."

The family. Brothers, wives, kids. Oh, God. Was she ready for this?

Chapter Sixteen

AFTER GLENNA LEFT, Mitch and Dylan sat down at the wooden kitchen table. The table was big, large enough for twelve or more. The housekeeper, Glory, had laid out an array of cold cuts, breads, condiments, chips, and last but definitely not least in Mitch's eyes, two pies and a chocolate cake.

"Might as well eat something. I'm not sure how long Glory and Glenna will be," Dylan said. They each loaded up a plate and took it to the table.

Mitch took a few bites and sighed. He'd forgotten what good American cooking tasted like. "This is great. Thanks."

"Thank Glory. Oh, and don't forget to eat some dessert. They're all homemade. Glory thinks anyone who won't eat her desserts is sick. I can't really argue."

"Don't worry," Mitch told him. "I'll do my part."

After they'd eaten their sandwiches and each had a dessert, they started talking again before Glenna returned.

"She looks like Glenna, but..." Dylan shrugged. "She doesn't remember anything, does she?"

"Very little, as far as I can tell," Mitch said. "Fragments. Bits and pieces. But that's it." He didn't add that she remembered less about her family than she did about Argentina. The man already felt bad enough. No need to rub it in. Mitch tried to imagine what he'd feel like if his own brother, Austin, couldn't remember who he was. He couldn't. It was hard enough to see Dylan going through it. "I can give you a full account of what happened whenever you want."

"My brothers should be here before long. Might as well wait so you don't have to go through it more than once."

"Probably best that way. Especially for Glenna." Once was going to be hard enough.

"Do you think she's up to it?" Dylan asked. "She seems kind of fragile." He got up and paced a few steps. "It's weird," he continued. "Glenna's always been so strong. Strong-willed. Sure of herself."

Thinking about how she'd handled herself in some very dicey situations, Mitch laughed. "She still is, most of the time. She's had to deal with some bad shit and has done better than ninety-nine out of a hundred people would have." He sobered. "But the amnesia has pretty well blown her world apart. She'll be okay one minute and then she'll get real quiet and you can tell she's trying to remember something. And failing. I don't think she's accustomed to failure."

Dylan smiled ruefully. "No, failing isn't part of Glenna's

makeup."

"Gee, isn't that good to know." Glenna strode into the room with Glory following behind. "I'm here now so you can stop talking *about* me and talk *to* me."

"Settle down, Freckles," Dylan said.

"Freckles?"

"That's what we used to call you when you went on a tear." He sighed. "But you don't recognize it, do you?"

"No. I'm sorry."

"You don't need to say you're sorry about everything. Just tell us when you do remember something."

Glory, who had busied herself making a plate, said, "Here you are, Glenna. I gave you a bit of everything. Do you want tea or something else?"

"Tea sounds good. Thank you." She took her plate, sat next to Mitch, and started eating. Glory brought her a glass of tea, then left them, saying she had to take care of something.

"Why are you staring at me, Dylan?" Glenna asked him when she had eaten some of her food. "Do I look that different?"

"No, but I haven't seen you in five years. I'm having a hard time believing you're here."

"Do you know why I haven't been back in so long? Mitch and Glory mentioned a fight with my father. But that doesn't explain what happened later, after he was gone."

"We don't know for sure. You came for Dad's funeral

but you left right after. You claimed you had to get back to work. Which was probably true. You managed the Villareal ranch and it happened during your busy season."

"Why didn't I come back after that?"

"I don't know. You always claimed you were too busy to leave. But we corresponded a lot. Then a few months ago, you suddenly quit answering my letters. And you never would use email. Again, we don't know why."

"Maybe I quit corresponding because I was ashamed," Glenna said.

"Ashamed of what?" Dylan asked. "None of us believe you embezzled money from the Villareals."

Mitch frowned but kept his mouth shut. Even though he didn't believe the cattle business debacle was wholly Glenna's fault, he didn't know what Dylan and the rest of her family thought about it. And whatever that was, Glenna needed to deal with it.

"I'm afraid the cattle business failed because of me. Which would mean I'm incompetent and that would give me a great reason not to want to talk to my family."

Dylan shook his head decisively. "Glenna, I don't believe you're incompetent any more than I believe you embezzled money. First off, you managed the business for several years successfully. There had to be a reason it cratered, since apparently that happened before the disease wiped out the herd. Maybe it failed because the Villareals lost the money through bad investments, or gambling, or something we're not even thinking about."

"I can dig deeper into that if you want," Mitch said. "Dylan's right. There could be any number of reasons the business failed that had nothing to do with you."

"What if the Villareals led you to believe the failure was your fault, but in reality it was theirs, and you found out?" Dylan asked.

"I guess it could have happened that way," she said doubtfully.

"Damn right it could have." Dylan looked out the window. "Shit. What have those damn dogs gotten into this time?" He opened the kitchen door, saying over his shoulder, "I'll be back. Gotta take care of something."

They heard him calling, "Mike, Ike, you get back here right now!"

"I wonder what they've done," Glenna said. She picked up her plate and carried it to the sink.

"No idea," Mitch said, following her. "Are you all right?" He leaned back against the sink with his arms crossed over his chest.

"Do you want the truth or a bullshit answer?"

"Truth."

"I think I'm having a panic attack, and that makes me feel like a shit. Not only because of the panic but because of what it's doing to Dylan and Glory to know I remember nothing. When the others get here it will be even worse."

"First of all, stop spinning your wheels over something

you can't help. It's not your fault you have amnesia, so stop acting like it is. No one else is blaming you."

"That's not what I'm doing."

"Isn't it?"

"You're leaving, aren't you? After you talk to my brothers."

That came out of left field. "I'm going to see my brother, yeah."

"Are you staying with him?"

Mitch shrugged. "He's got a one-bedroom apartment, so no. I'll get a hotel room."

"Take me with you. Please."

MITCH SIMPLY STARED at her. She knew she sounded crazy to him, but she couldn't help it. "Just for a little while," she added desperately. "Until I can get a grip on the situation."

"Glenna, you know I can't do that. It will kill your family if you don't stay here. You'll be all right."

"No, I won't. If you won't let me come with you, will you stay here? There's plenty of room. I think."

"What's going on? You weren't this upset after the first attempted kidnapping." He turned her to face him, both hands on her arms. "What's got you so spooked?"

Unable to explain, she shook her head.

"Look at me, Glenna." She raised her gaze to his eyes.

He searched her face. "Damn." He bent his head down

and kissed her.

Glenna wrapped her arms around his waist and kissed him back.

Someone cleared his throat. "Don't let us interrupt," one of her brothers said.

Wyatt. She knew it was him because of his blond hair, and obviously, she knew Dylan, who stood behind him. But she wasn't sure about the one who walked in last. He had sandy brown hair. Except for hair color, they all resembled each other. "We won't," she said, holding on to Mitch even as he dropped his hands.

Poker face, Glenna thought, glancing at Mitch. She'd seen that expression before and still had no clue what he was thinking.

Though she'd turned to face the three men, she held on to Mitch's hand. They had a little tug of war, which she won. "You're Wyatt," she said, pointing to the blond. She paused, and looked at the other one.

"Sean," he said, his mouth kicking up in a smile. "And you're Glenna."

"That's what they tell me." She let go of Mitch's hand.

Sean chuckled. "Yeah, you're Glenna. You always were a smartass. Good to know some things haven't changed."

"What hasn't changed?" asked Jack, entering the kitchen from the back door.

"Glenna's still a smartass," Dylan said.

Jack walked over and simply looked at her for a long

RETURN OF THE COWGIRL

moment. She gazed back at him, wondering if the flash of recognition she felt was real or simply imagined. Then Jack smiled, pulled her into his arms and hugged her. He released her and said, "I know you don't remember me but I remember you and there's no way I'm not hugging my little sister. So deal with it."

That broke the ice as much as anything. She had to laugh and then be hugged by all her brothers. It wasn't nearly as weird as she'd thought it might be.

"Might as well sit in here. I see apple pie calling my name," Sean said.

They all picked a dessert and took it to the table. Glenna was glad for the easy acceptance she felt from her brothers. They didn't act like there was anything strange about Glenna being back after so long, and with amnesia on top of it. Their attitude made her feel...well, normal. Which at this point was a great feeling.

"Are you up for telling us what happened, Glenna?"

"I can only tell you what happened after the bus accident. Mitch will have to tell you the rest, and what we pieced together since.

"Before we get started, Glory needs to hear this too," Sean said. "Where is she?"

"I'll go get her," Dylan said and left the room.

"While we're waiting for Glory..." Wyatt said, turning to Glenna. "So, you and Mitch."

"No," Glenna said before Mitch could speak. "There is

no Mitch and me, although I'd like for there to be."

"Jesus, Glenna," Mitch said.

"What? It's not like you don't know it." Having effectively silenced him, she turned back to her brothers. "Mitch and I aren't together. Yet," she added with a meaningful glance at Mitch.

"It sure as hell looked like it when we came in." Wyatt said. "I'm thinking you move awfully fast, Mitch. Especially given that Glenna here has amnesia."

Before Glenna could come to Mitch's defense, Jack spoke up. "What are you talking about?"

"When we came in Glenna and Mitch were in a lip lock," Sean told him.

"Oh, yeah?" Jack gave Mitch a look that didn't bode well for him. Again, she wanted to defend him.

"Relax," Mitch said. "Nothing has happened and nothing is going to happen."

"I wouldn't be too sure of that," Dylan said, entering the kitchen with Glory close behind him.

"What's this about?" Glory asked.

"Lip lock. Jack's playing oldest brother, Mitch is denying anything is going on and Glenna is bound and determined there is going to be." Dylan looked at Glenna. "Does that about cover it?"

"Mostly. Mitch thinks because I have amnesia he has to treat me like I'm made of glass and that I don't know what I'm doing because I'm still not sure who I am. But I do.

Know what I'm doing, that is."

Mitch stood, grabbed her hand and none too gently, yanked her up. "Excuse us," he said. "We'll be back."

He dragged her into the library and shut the door.

"I haven't seen this room yet," Glenna said. "What a cool room." The room was nothing fancy, but there were bookshelves on every wall and even one below the window, crammed with books of every variety. Paperback, hardback, nonfiction, fiction. Before she could inspect them further, Mitch backed her up against the door and caged her in with his hands on either side of her face. Her heart rate sped up the longer he looked at her.

"I don't know whether to kiss you or strangle you."

"Kissing is a lot more fun, don't you think?"

He cupped her face in his hands and tilted her head back. And then he kissed her. A long, slow, drugging kiss. A sultry duel of tongues and teeth and lips. By the time he pulled away her legs felt like jelly.

"I guess this means you're not mad at me?"

"No. It just means I can't resist you. And I should. Hell, Glenna, you don't know anything about your past and damn little about me."

"That's not true. I know a lot about you. You saved me from kidnappers at least twice. You dragged me around with you for days and you never laid a hand on me except to hug me when I asked you to. Even though we were together 24/7 and it was obvious I wouldn't have stopped you. I know everything I need to know."

He leaned his forehead against hers. "Much as I'd like to stay here, I'm sure your brothers are ready to draw and quarter me by now."

"I'm a grown woman. They have no say in this." She put her arms around his neck, pulled his head down to hers and kissed him.

Chapter Seventeen

ORDINARILY, MITCH WASN'T the nervous type. But he
had to admit that walking into a room with four men
and a woman who probably wanted to take him apart wasn't
anything he looked forward to. Glenna took everything into
her hands, though.

"I'm just putting this out there," she announced when
they walked in. "I'm a grown woman. Yes, I have amnesia.
Yes, I know what I want. Do not give Mitch or me any shit.
Got it?"

There was a blonde woman standing by Dylan who
laughed and stepped forward. "Hi, Glenna. Hi, Mitch," she
said shaking hands. "I'm Sam, Dylan's fiancée. I can't
guarantee they'll listen, but you sure made an impression."

"Let's go in the living room," Dylan said. "It will be
more comfortable."

"Everyone wanted to meet you, Glenna, but we were
afraid the whole crew would be a little overwhelming the first
day you were home," Jack said. "The rest of the family will
be here tomorrow night for dinner."

"So, Mitch, fill us in," Wyatt said. "Dylan told us the basic story, but I understand there's more."

Mitch went through the story again, briefly, about how he'd found Glenna and convinced her of her identity. Then he went into more detail. "We believe the kidnapping attempts were undertaken by Villareal hired thugs. Besides the first attempt, when they tried to snatch her off the street, they broke into my hotel room in Valparaiso. I recognized one of them, so I know it was the same people. And once we discovered the counterfeit cash, it seemed logical that's the reason they came after us."

"There could be another reason too," Glenna said. "I think Rolando might be after me because of something else."

"What's that?" Sean said.

She exchanged a glance with Mitch. "It's up to you," he said.

"I think I was involved with Rolando Villareal. He claims we're married. Mitch's secretary couldn't find anything out about a marriage but I was definitely involved with someone before I left the ranch."

"How do you know that?" Wyatt asked. "Did you remember something?"

"No." She shook her head. "When I woke up at the hospital in Zapala they told me I'd lost my baby."

"Damn. I'm sorry," Wyatt said.

"I'm so sorry, Glenna," Sam said. "I can't imagine how difficult that was."

"Like I told Mitch, I'm sure it would be if I could remember it. I had no idea I was pregnant, much less who the father was."

"But you think it was Villareal," Dylan said.

"It seems logical," Mitch said. "And if she was pregnant with his child, he'd come after her. Having an heir is still a huge deal in South America."

"And you don't know if he knew of your pregnancy, right?"

"Right. I was around five months along when I left, but according to the doctors in Zapala I wasn't showing significantly. So there's a chance he knew, but it's also possible he didn't. I'm not sure if the pregnancy is why I left or there was something else that made me leave. Whenever I try to think about the day I left, to see if I remember anything, I get sick and shaky."

"You didn't tell me that," Mitch said.

"It didn't seem important. I still didn't remember anything but fragments. The first time or two I tried to remember that day weren't too bad, but the more I tried to recall anything about the day I left, the worse it got. So I quit trying."

"I can see why," Sam said.

"I dream about things but I don't usually remember when I wake up. And what I do remember is all mixed up."

"Glenna, have you had time to see a doctor since you left that hospital?" Sam asked.

"She's seeing four of you now," Dylan said.

"Oh, you're funny," Sam told him, but it was obvious she was teasing. "I mean a doctor about your memory loss."

"Mitch said he'd ask his brother to see me."

"Austin Hardeman is a neurologist at the Marietta hospital. He's the one who recommended Mitch," Dylan told Glory, who'd been sitting very quietly taking in the conversation.

"Is Glenna safe here?" Glory asked. "What if this Villareal person comes looking for her here?"

Exactly what had Mitch worried. "It will be obvious pretty quickly if he does come to Marietta. I'd like to think the Argentine cops will bust their operation, but my friend Felix, the Chilean cop we gave the bills to, didn't have anything to tie those fake bills to the Villareals except our say-so." He shrugged. "They're just as likely to ignore us as to raid the Villareal ranch."

"So there's no other evidence about this counterfeiting operation?" Jack asked.

"We don't know. If there is, it's locked up tight in Glenna's mind until her memory returns." His phone rang. Checking the Caller ID, he saw it was Austin. "I need to take this." As he answered, he walked out of the room into the kitchen.

"Hey, Mitch. When did you get in?"

"A few hours ago. Are you off work?"

"I am. Come over when you're finished there and we'll

have a beer."

"Sounds good. It shouldn't be too much longer."

"Are you going to stay with me?"

Mitch laughed. "And sleep on your couch? I'll pass. I'll get a room at the Graff." He looked up to see Glenna in the kitchen doorway.

"I'll see you soon, then."

"Yeah. Later." He hung up and looked at Glenna.

"I didn't mean to interrupt," she said, walking up to him.

"You didn't. I'm about to leave, anyway."

"You're going to a hotel? Are you sure you won't stay here?"

"If I stay here you know what's going to happen."

She didn't pretend to misunderstand. "You think if you go to a hotel nothing's going to happen between us?"

"There's a lot better chance if I'm not here seeing you all day every day."

"Are you going to stay in Marietta a while, then?"

"Yes. I haven't seen my brother in quite a while."

"Is your brother the only reason you're staying?"

"You know damn good and well it's not."

"Do I?"

Mitch put his arms around her. He'd never held a woman in his arms before and felt so sure that she belonged there. "Yes," he said, and kissed her. He forced himself to end the kiss and let her go long before he wanted to.

"Will I see you tomorrow?"

"Yes." He should try to put some distance between them, but he couldn't talk himself into it. He told her family goodbye and that he was staying at the Graff and would be in town for a while. Then he left before he changed his mind and took Glenna with him.

MITCH HADN'T SEEN Austin in several months. His brother pretty much never came back to Texas and unless Mitch had no jobs in the offing, he didn't often get to Marietta. But he was here now and really glad to see his big brother. Austin was the only person in the world who Mitch trusted completely. Their parents had died in a private plane crash when Mitch was twenty and Austin twenty-two. Both of them had suddenly become multi-millionaires, heirs to the Hardeman Hardware empire.

Austin, possibly because he was just starting his medical residency and knew what he wanted to do with his life, had handled his sudden wealth a hell of a lot better than Mitch had.

But he wasn't here to think about the past. He needed to figure out the present. And what he was going to do about Glenna Gallagher. One thing was certain: he couldn't forget her.

"It's about damn time you came to see me," Austin said, after they'd hugged and pounded each other on the back.

"Says he who can't ever get his ass to Texas."

"I have patients."

"I have a job."

They both laughed. This exchange took place each time they saw each other after some time had passed. "Sit down and I'll get us a beer."

"Sounds good." He sat on the couch.

Austin came back in the room and handed him a beer, then popped the top on his and sat in the recliner. "Tell me about this job. I've told my office staff to work Glenna Gallagher in as soon as she calls."

"Thanks, I appreciate it. I don't know whether you can help her, but I trust you to either help her or find someone who can."

Austin rubbed his chin. "You realize three of her brothers are doctors, right? As well as Sam, her soon-to-be sister-in-law. They might want her to see someone else."

"Is there another neurologist here?"

"Yes, one other. And I think another one is coming."

"I don't know those other people. I do know you, and you know the Gallaghers. I don't see that it's a problem."

Glenna wasn't a job anymore. Not at all. He gave Austin a brief account of what had happened in South America, but as soon as he finished that, he stopped. What could he say?

"What's bothering you, Mitch?"

"*Who's* bothering me." Mitch got up and paced around. Shoved his hand through his hair and turned to look at his brother. "It's Glenna. She's not just a job."

145

"I kind of gathered that," his brother said dryly.

"Glenna is...different. From the moment I met her she hasn't been what I expected. For the first time since Eliana suckered me, I found a woman who is totally guileless."

"That's good, isn't it?"

He squeezed the bridge of his nose. "I don't know. You know my track record with women."

"Are you talking about when you were young, stupid and thinking with your dick? Or are you talking about all the women since? Every one of them young, pretty, and mostly brainless."

"Either. Both. I don't know."

"What does she look like?"

He took out the picture he'd carried around when he was looking for her and gave it to Austin. He studied it for a bit. "She's pretty." He handed the picture back to Mitch.

"No, she's beautiful. In this picture—" he waved it around "—she's pretty. In real life she's drop-dead gorgeous."

"Have you slept with her?"

Mitch stopped pacing long enough to glare at his brother. "Have you not been listening to me? The woman has amnesia. She doesn't know anything about herself. Hell, she didn't know her real name until I told her and convinced her. Which wasn't easy, by the way. I'm not some perv taking advantage of her."

Austin laughed. "You're a lot of things, Mitch. But a perv, you are not. It's obvious you're hot for her. Does she feel the same?"

He shrugged. "She thinks she does. But shit, she doesn't know if she's married or involved or in love with this Rolando asshole or if she's scared to death and running from him. She doesn't know if he's a criminal or simply caught up in something against his will." He thought about that a minute. "My money's on him being central to this scheme."

"So you don't plan to sleep with Glenna until that's all straightened out? Until she gets her memory back or you find out if she's married and exactly what these people want from her?"

Mitch shot him an annoyed glance. "I have no idea what I'm going to do. I know what I should do, at least until we know more."

"Leave her alone?" Austin asked.

Mitch nodded. "Yeah. I should walk away. For now, anyway."

"Let me know how well that works out."

Probably not at all, he admitted to himself. "Glenna's— She doesn't know enough about herself to lie. I'm not sure she would even if she did have her memory."

"Whoa, Mitch Hardeman admitting there might be a woman in the world who's not after his money? Must be love."

He knew Austin was expecting him to deny it. Vehemently. But he couldn't. "She doesn't know a damn thing about my money." Thankfully, Eliana hadn't gotten everything because some of it had been in trust. So he had a lean few years before the trust dissolved. He got up and paced. "I don't know what it is."

"I was kidding."

"I'm not. I think I'm in love with her. I haven't even known her for a week. How can I be in love with her? That's crazy." It was about sex. Forced proximity. That's all.

Austin raised his eyebrows. "How does she feel about you?"

"She wants to see where it goes. But how can I do that when she's got goddamn amnesia? I'm the only person she knows. The only person she trusts."

"That's a heavy responsibility."

"Yeah, but that isn't what I'm afraid of. What if I let her down? What if she figures out she's still in love with her baby daddy?"

"What if she's not? What if she's falling for you and would have no matter whether she has her memory or not? She sounds like she's a decisive woman normally."

"She is. And resourceful. She managed to elude me and Villareal's flunkies for weeks. That's not easy to do." He finished his beer and thought briefly about having another. He didn't though. The lesson he'd learned years ago had stayed with him. "What are you smiling about?" he asked Austin.

"Just thinking that you're toast."

Damn it, he couldn't even deny it.

Chapter Eighteen

G LENNA WOKE EARLY the next day and went down to the kitchen. Glory stood at the kitchen island, making breakfast, and Dylan and Sam sat at the big table with coffee and their tablets. Both of them were dressed. Dylan in jeans and a T-shirt, Sam in light blue scrubs.

Dylan's fiancée was a very pretty blonde. Since she was a trauma surgeon Glenna had thought she would be intimidating, but she wasn't. She was warm and friendly and easy to talk to. Still, Glenna had heard her talking to someone at the hospital the night before and she had no doubt that Sam was a strong, confident woman who didn't take shit from anyone. She wasn't sure why she knew that. Sam hadn't sounded rude or angry, but there was a core of steel in her voice when talking medicine. Which was a good thing in a trauma surgeon, Glenna thought.

"Hey. Did you have a good night?" Dylan asked, looking up.

"I did. Thanks."

"Coffee's over there," Sam said, motioning in Glory's

general direction. "I've got to get going," she added as she got up and kissed Dylan goodbye.

"You take a breakfast bar with you," Glory said.

Sam laughed. "You don't have to tell me twice. Those things are great." To Glenna she said, "Have fun today. I'll see you later."

"Everything is on the stove," Glory announced. "Except the muffins and they're on the counter." She left the kitchen, headed for the laundry room, if Glenna remembered correctly from the quick tour she'd had the day before.

"Did you have plans for today?" Dylan asked Glenna.

"I was planning on calling the neurologist for an appointment, but other than that, no. Why?"

"I could use some help with the horses."

"I don't—" She started to say she didn't know anything about horses, but according to everything she'd heard, she did know horses. "All right."

"You don't remember, do you?"

"No. I'm sor—"

"I told you not to apologize," Dylan interrupted. "Sam put some clothes and boots in your room that she thinks will fit you. After we eat we can go see the horses." He paused and added, "The stalls need to be mucked out. That was always one of your favorite jobs."

She narrowed her eyes at him. "I think you're the one shoveling shit. I can't believe I liked mucking out stalls."

Dylan laughed and went to get his breakfast. "Hey, I figured it was worth a try."

"I have amnesia," she said, following suit. "I'm not stu-pid."

"How was I to know you remembered what mucking out stalls means?"

She tilted her head, considering him. "Were you always this way?"

"What way?" he asked innocently.

"A pain in the ass."

He laughed again. "It's one of my most endearing quali-ties."

"That's not how I'd describe it," she said dryly.

After they finished eating, Glenna went up to change. Sam and Glenna were about the same height and size, so Sam's clothes fit her well. The boots were a little big, but not enough that she couldn't wear them. She made a mental note to thank Sam.

She'd told Dylan she'd meet him at the stables. About halfway there, the dogs came out to greet her. She counted eight and wondered if there were more. Apparently, Dylan liked dogs as well as horses.

At the round pen she stopped to watch Dylan with a beautiful stallion. He was a buckskin with dark stockings and a long, flowing black and white mane. "What's his name?" she called out.

"Trouble. He's my new stud."

A stud. Volcán. A magnificent Criollo stallion, coal black with white socks and a white stripe on his nose. Beautiful. Wild. Hers to tame.

She shook off the memory, if you could call something that fleeting a memory. "He's gorgeous," she told Dylan. "What type of horse is he?"

"Norwegian Fjord. I've been raising them for a while now."

"Do they all have manes like his?"

"They're all black and white, but the others are short. I'll show you when we go down to the pasture. I'm about to put Trouble out."

"Why is he named Trouble?"

"That was his name when I got him. He'd been abused and he was hell to get to trust us. Although he fell for Sam right away."

"Did you?" she asked curiously.

His smile was pure happiness. "Yep. Took one look at her and I was a goner."

She smiled too, thinking how both his voice and his expression had changed when he talked about his fiancée.

"And so did Trouble," Dylan continued. "Pretty well everyone falls for Sam. Come on, we'll go down to the pasture and I'll tell you about the horses."

"I'd like that."

Dylan opened the gate to the round pen and led the stallion out. "Want to pet him? He doesn't bite…anymore."

Glenna gave him a dirty look but went ahead and patted

Trouble. Luckily, he was perfectly well behaved. Something about the horse and the smells associated with the round pen and drifting over from the barn seemed familiar. "Do you have any horses who were here when I lived here?"

"A few. Mercy's been around a long time. I'll call her over when we get to the pasture."

Mercy was an older mare, a quarter horse, Dylan said. She came to Dylan immediately when he called her. The mare was buttermilk buckskin with a black star on her forehead, black stockings, and a black mane and tail. How had she known what to call that color? She'd remembered. Maybe having her memory return wasn't hopeless after all.

"She's so sweet," Glenna said, petting her. "Aren't you a love?" she crooned to the mare.

"Do you want to ride? Mercy's not fast anymore but she's a sweetheart. She might be just what you need. But I'm betting riding comes back to you, even if the people and horses don't yet."

"I hope so." But she wasn't at all sure it would, despite her memory of the Criollo stallion and just now about the buttermilk buckskin. Yet when she went with Dylan to get the tack, she reached for the correct bridle, and when she helped him saddle the horses, she knew instinctively what to do. Watching him saddle his own horse after that, a gelding he called Hawkeye, seemed like a familiar task, too. She didn't want to place too much importance on what had taken place, but she couldn't help being encouraged.

They didn't ride for long, just long enough to get some fresh air and see a bit of the ranch. Dylan took her to a stream he called Lover's Creek and they followed it along for a while. "Why is it called Lover's Creek?" she asked.

"The story goes that our great-grandfather proposed to our great-grandmother there. At least that's one version."

"What's the other one?"

"Our grandmother swore our father was conceived somewhere along the creek."

Glenna laughed. "She sounds colorful."

"Oh, she was. She was a no-nonsense rancher's wife who worked hard her whole life. But she had a wicked sense of humor. She especially enjoyed telling that story around some of the stuffier 'town folk' as she called them."

It seemed like as good a time as any to ask about other family members. "Speaking of our father, tell me about him. Do you know why I left the ranch so young?"

"Not really." He shrugged. "We always suspected it had something to do with his hardheaded attitude about women doing 'men's work'." He made air quotes. "You wouldn't put up with that and you set about proving you could do anything the rest of us could do."

"Could I?"

He grinned. "Yeah. With the exception of a few things I don't think you wanted to do anyway."

"What were those?" she asked curiously.

He turned Hawkeye back toward the barn. "Bull riding,

steer wrestling, and steer roping. And you hid when we gelded anything. You didn't even like to take the dogs and cats to get them neutered or spayed, even though you knew it was necessary."

"What happened to our mother? No one ever talks about her."

"She died when you and I were little. I was six. You were seven. She had cancer. I don't remember a lot, but her death hit everyone hard." He glanced at her and smiled. "You decided I needed a mother, so you tried to fulfill that role."

"Did you mind?" It was hard to visualize the confident adult he was now as a little boy of six who'd lost his mother.

"Not most of the time. Sometimes you annoyed the crap out of me, though."

Glenna laughed. "Well, that's good to know. I'm sure you deserved it."

"I imagine I did." He smiled, then sobered. "Anyway, about Dad. After he died, you came back for the funeral but wouldn't stay for the reading of the will. When we heard what was in it, we figured that was what the fight was about."

"Mitch told me about that. I had to marry before I turned thirty-one or my share got split among the four of you. That pisses me off even now when I don't remember him. Not because I care about the inheritance," she added hastily. "But it's the principle of the thing."

"You clashed, that's for sure. You were a lot like him.

Maybe that's why you didn't get along. He was a good father, at least to us boys. But he had his faults. Like everyone does, I guess."

After they returned, Glenna helped Dylan cool down the horses and put them back in the pasture. "Thanks for taking me riding. I really enjoyed it. Some of it even felt familiar."

"That's good."

Good, but it still didn't mean she'd ever remember everything. Or even most of her life. "Have you heard of anyone around town needing a waitress? Or a sales clerk or something similar?"

"No, why?"

"Because I need a job and I don't know what I can do. But I'm pretty sure I could manage something like that." Although she might be a crummy waitress. Probably would be. Still, she could try if it meant work.

"Work with me. I always need help and maybe being around the horses will help you to remember."

"Thanks, Dylan, but I need a paying job."

"Why?"

"Because I don't have any money, duh," she snapped.

"What about—" He broke off. "I guess you can't get at your money in Argentina, huh?"

"Not now, anyway. Maybe never."

"You have your portion of the ranch."

"How can I have a portion of the ranch if I'm not married?"

"Mitch said you might be married to that Rolando asshole."

"Might being the operative word. Mitch and his assistant haven't found any record of a marriage. Besides, I hope to God I'm not married to him." She had a number of reasons she didn't want to be married to Rolando Villareal, not the least of which were Mitch Hardeman and the minor detail that Villareal was almost certainly a criminal.

"It doesn't really matter. Jack, Sean, Wyatt and I decided a long time ago that if you ever came back to stay you were entitled to your portion of the ranch and the money Dad left."

"That's very sweet of all of you, but no. I'm not taking anything he didn't want me to have."

Dylan shook his head. "Damn, you may not remember, but that was exactly what I'd expect you to say. And by the way, don't be a stubborn ass about it."

"I'm not being a stubborn ass," she said, stung.

Dylan crossed his arms over his chest and raised an eyebrow. "Oh, really? If it walks like a duck…"

"Ha, ha. You are so not funny."

"I know you're gonna do what you're gonna do, but think about working here." He held up his hand before she could protest again. "I'll pay you, same as I would anyone who works for me."

Slightly mollified, she said, "All right. I'll think about it." Maybe she should take him up on the offer. It just occurred to her that if she worked in town, she'd see a lot of people who had known Glenna Gallagher. It was doubtful she'd remember any of them. Which meant she'd have to explain—multiple times—that she wasn't being a snot, she had amnesia.

Ugh. Not something she wanted to do. Working for Dylan was looking better and better.

MITCH HAD DEBATED the wisdom of seeing Glenna again so soon but when she called and asked when he was coming to see her, he'd gotten in his rental car and driven out to the Gallagher ranch.

He parked by the house and walked down to the stables where she'd said to meet her. Glenna stood by the round pen with her back to him, her hair in a single long braid down her back. The horse was a beauty, a buckskin with dark stockings and a black and white mane. As he drew near, she turned around and a smile spread like sunshine over her face. He was struck once again by how beautiful she was.

"Hey," she said. "I'm glad you came."

"Hey. How are you?" After propping a foot on the rail, he glanced around, then back at her. "You look like you belong here. Or at least, on a ranch."

"I seem to know something about horses. Dylan took me riding this morning."

"How was that?"

"Nice. Really nice. He told me some family history too."

"You feeling a little better about things?"

"A little. Still can't remember much of anything. I made an appointment today with your brother. He's squeezing me in tomorrow."

"Good. He said he'd told his staff to clear a spot for you whenever you called." The horse snorted, walked up to Glenna and hung his head over the fence. She rubbed his forehead and down to his muzzle. The stallion nickered at her, tossed his head and looked disappointed at finding nothing in her hands. "I'm sorry, Trouble. I don't have anything for you."

"Trouble?"

"Dylan's new stud. Dylan says the horse was pretty wild when he got him. He thinks he was abused. But Dylan and Sam have been working with him and he's improved a lot." She looked at him. "Do you like horses?"

He hid a grin. "What would you think if I didn't?"

"I'm reserving judgment. Pat him. But be careful. He bites."

"Is this a test? What happens if he bites me?"

"I imagine it will hurt like shit."

He let his grin loose at that. He moved even closer to Glenna, reached for Trouble and patted his cheek. The stallion eyed him cautiously, but apparently decided Mitch wasn't worth biting.

"You do like horses. I thought so."

"My brother and I had horses when we were young." Until after their parents died and neither Austin nor Mitch could give them or the farm the attention it needed. They'd sold it and the horses to their long-time foreman and family. Mitch still visited the family from time to time.

"Do you want to ride sometime?"

"I don't know. Depends on how long I'm here."

"About that. Can I ask you something?"

"Sure." But he said it warily.

"Are you going to give us a chance? Stick around for a while?"

How was he supposed to answer that? He wanted to. In fact, it shocked him how much he wanted to be with her. His feelings about Glenna were complicated by so many things, not the least of which was her amnesia. But one thing wasn't complex at all. He wanted her. Wanted to hold her, kiss her, fill his hands with her breasts and feel her wrapped around him as he sank inside her. Wanted to kiss her and swallow her cries as she came apart in his arms.

"You're looking at me like you want to…"

"I do," he said roughly. "But it's still not happening."

"Because I have amnesia."

"Yeah. Because of that."

She gave him a long look, then shrugged. "Okay."

Okay? What the hell did that mean? Something told him she hadn't accepted his decision as final, but her response sure made it seem like she did.

Chapter Nineteen

LATER THAT DAY Glenna looked at the time on her phone. The burner phone Dylan had given her, insisting it was a welcome home present. She drew in a deep breath. With her door cracked open she could hear voices coming from the living room. The family—*her family*—was here.

There was no reason to be nervous. She'd met all of her brothers and Sam yesterday. Tonight she would meet the rest of the wives and the kids. All the kids were Jack's and Maya's but Wyatt's wife, Mia, was pregnant. Dylan had filled her in on the family when they were cooling down the horses. She hoped she could remember all the names, but it sounded like a lot of people were coming. She wished one of them was Mitch but he'd flat-out refused, telling her she didn't need an outsider with her when she met all of her family for the first time.

Glenna wore her jeans and one of the blouses Sam had loaned her. It was a pretty, pale blue tunic top. She wrapped a brown belt, also Sam's, around her waist and figured that was as good as she got. She wavered between her running shoes, which looked really bad, and Sam's boots, which were a little too big. Settling on the too big boots, she decided she'd have to bite the bullet and borrow some money to buy new shoes, if nothing else. She already owed her brothers for flying her from Chile to the US, what was a little more?

Glenna wound up having a much better time than she'd imagined. The Gallaghers were obviously close. All of them—men, women and children—got along surprisingly well. Or else they were putting on a show for her, but she didn't think so.

When she walked into the living room they were discussing Dylan and Sam's wedding.

"Who's going to be your best man, Dylan?" Jack asked. He was holding his baby son and was busy making faces at him. The baby laughed happily.

"You'll find out." Dylan took a sip of his beer.

"Yeah, but when? You haven't asked me or Sean or Wyatt. Has he?" He turned to his other brothers.

"Not me," Sean said.

"Me either. The wedding is in a couple of weeks," Wyatt said. "What are you waiting for?"

Dylan looked across the room and exchanged a smile with Sam. "Don't worry. I've got it under control."

It struck her forcibly that these people really liked each other. They joked and kidded but she could see that they enjoyed being around each other. Maya, Jack's wife, had been his high school sweetheart, so here was another person she was supposed to know. When she met Mia, Wyatt's wife, the first thing she said to Glenna was, "Don't worry. You don't know me."

"Thank God," Glenna said fervently. Mia let out a peal of laughter. Glenna winced. "I didn't mean that like it sounded."

"It sounded like you're overwhelmed and who could blame you?" She grabbed the arm of an absolutely stunning woman with long black hair. "This is Honey, Sean's wife. Sorry, but you do know her."

Honey looked at Mia quizzically before turning to Glenna. "Am I missing something?" she asked Glenna.

"Only me putting my foot in my mouth."

Eyes dancing, Mia said, "When I told Glenna she didn't know me she said, 'Thank God'."

They all laughed. Glenna took the ribbing in the spirit it was intended. In fact, it made her feel a little less uncomfortable and more like family. "I'm never going to live that down, am I?"

"Oh, I'm sure you're not," Honey said. "You have to admit it's too good of a story not to tell."

"Have you told Glenna how you and Sean met?"

Honey shook her head. "We met several years before but he didn't remember. I was dating Dylan at the time."

"That sounds like a story."

Before Honey could answer, Mia did. "She dropped into

Sean's arms. Literally."

"This I have to hear," Glenna said.

Honey told the story and then convinced Mia to tell Glenna about hers and Wyatt's romance. It was impossible not to like them. All of them. She held the baby and played with him until he started crying and then she found herself giving him a bottle. The two teenagers, Carmen and Gina, belonged to Jack and Maya. They came over while she was feeding the baby and talked to her.

"Aunt Glenna?"

Wow, she was an aunt. She hadn't really thought about it until one of the girls called her that. "You're Gina, right?"

She laughed. "No, I'm Carmen."

"Carmen. Then you must be Gina," she said to the other girl. "Call me Glenna. Aunt Glenna makes me feel old."

"Do you speak Spanish super well, Glenna?" Gina asked.

"Yes, I'm bilingual." Which she hadn't known until Mitch spoke to her in English. She wondered if she'd have ever remembered she spoke English if he hadn't. "Why?"

"We're both taking Spanish and we suck. We wondered if you'd help us."

"I'd be happy to. My Spanish might be a bit different from what you're learning, though, since I speak an Argentine dialect. It's called *Rioplatense*."

"But it's mostly the same, right?" Carmen clarified.

"I think some of it is," Glenna answered with a smile. "But honestly, I'm not an expert on Spanish dialects."

"It would be cool to learn some, though. Will you still teach us?"

Glenna laughed. "Sure."

After they left her, Jack came over to sit beside her. "How are you? Really, not the platitudes you think we want to hear."

She answered honestly. "It's a mixed bag. Everyone is being so great. They're kind and inclusive and it makes me feel like a shit that I can't remember anyone."

Jack smiled. "It's not as if it's a choice, Glenna. Don't expect too much out of yourself. None of us is holding you to a timetable."

"Mitch is."

"What do you mean?"

She frowned. "I'm afraid he's going to leave Marietta before I ever get my memory back."

"And that would be bad because…"

"Because I don't want him to leave. You can probably tell that I have feelings for Mitch."

"I did get that impression," Jack said dryly.

"Yes, apparently I'm not one to hide how I feel." Or what she wanted.

"You never did. You haven't changed in that department. That's a good thing," he added.

"I'm glad you think so because I'm fairly sure I can't change it. I think Mitch has feelings for me, but he won't do anything because he doesn't want to *take advantage* of me.

Which I've told him is pure bullshit."

"You probably don't want to hear this, but it speaks highly of Mitch. There are a number of men who wouldn't care."

Maybe so, but it sure didn't help her dilemma.

"Have you thought about what you'll do when you do get your memory back? What if you're married, like the Villareals are claiming?"

"Yes, I've thought about it a lot. If I'm married to Rolando Villareal then I'm getting a divorce, immediately. He's a criminal and I was scared enough of him to run away."

"I won't argue with you about that. None of us want you to stay married to a criminal."

"I've also thought about what I'll do if my memory never comes back. I have to get on with my life. I can't wait forever for something that might never happen."

"You know we would all love to have you stay in Marietta. But if you decide to go somewhere else, we'll support your decision."

"Thank you. I appreciate that." She tilted her head, studying him. "Are you always this calm and logical?"

"Most of the time," he said with a grin. "With my patients. Not always with my family. But Maya made me promise to be reasonable and realize that you're a grown woman who's perfectly capable of making up her own mind."

"Even if that mind happens to have amnesia?"

"Even then."

"You're a good brother, Jack."

Dylan walked up in time to hear her comment. "He is. When he's not being a pain in the ass."

Jack gave him a narrow-eyed stare. "Do I need to remind you who helped you mend fences the last time you couldn't con anyone else into it?"

"Oh, yeah. I forgot about that," Dylan said with a wink at Glenna. "Jack is never a pain in the ass," he announced.

"And don't you forget it," Jack said.

GLENNA BORROWED A car and refused company to go see the neurologist, preferring to hear what the doctor said by herself. Maybe it was stupid, considering most of her family were doctors of some sort, but she felt it was something she needed to do on her own. She did put her brothers on the list of people her doctor could talk to about her appointment. Not that Dr. Hardeman would tell them anything he didn't tell her.

Dr. Austin Hardeman looked a lot like his brother, Mitch. His hair wasn't as dark and his eyes were a beautiful clear blue, but they were about the same height and their features were similar. In other words, he was a really fine-looking man.

Glenna didn't know what to expect from a neurological

exam. He tested her reflexes, her eyesight, and her hearing. He had her walk up and down the hall in several different ways. She had no idea what a few of the procedures were supposed to tell him. Then she had to get a number of other tests done, including an MRI of her brain. After the MRI she saw the doctor again, this time in his office rather than in an exam room.

"The good news is your neurological tests were all normal," Dr. Hardeman said. "I put a rush on the MRI results, but it depends on how busy they are as to when I'll get them back. However, I don't expect the MRI to show us anything we don't already know."

"So what's the bad news?"

"We have no way of knowing when or if your memory will return."

Even though she'd been expecting similar news, she felt a rush of disappointment. Part of her had been hoping for a miracle cure. "That sucks."

He nodded. "Yes. I'm sorry I don't have better news. However, I believe you will remember most of your life prior to the accident. Probably not what happened immediately before or even days or weeks before, but eventually you will remember. In the case of an injury like yours, most people do regain their memory. It's just impossible to predict when."

"Should I try to see a psychiatrist?"

"I can refer you to one, but given that your amnesia is

due to physical trauma, it's unlikely a psychiatrist can help you. On the other hand, it can't hurt."

"I'll think about it. Can I call your office for the referral if that's the way I decide to go?"

"Absolutely."

She stewed about it on the way home. For now she wouldn't try to see a psychiatrist, but if her memory loss persisted she might change her mind. She parked in the back and walked into the kitchen. There was no sign of Glory or anyone else, for that matter. Which was a little strange since Glory was almost always around at lunchtime.

Glenna sat at the big table and tried to decide if she should call Mitch and tell him what his brother had said, as unsatisfying as it was.

"You look upset," Sam said, coming into the kitchen with a pile of mail. Setting it down on the counter, she walked to the table. "Do you want to talk about it?"

"No, but I'll have to sometime. Maybe you could tell the rest of them. You know, the family." She thought about that. "No, that's a chickenshit way to handle it. Never mind. I'll tell them later."

"I take it your doctor's appointment didn't go well." Sam took a seat beside her.

Glenna shrugged. "About like I thought it would. After Dr. Hardeman examined me, he said my neurological tests were all normal. He doesn't know when he'll get the results of the MRI but he said he didn't expect any surprises from it."

"Glenna, that's good news."

"I suppose it is. But he also said I'd just have to wait and see when my memory would come back. If it does."

Sam patted her hand. "I'm sorry. That must have been hard to hear."

Glenna nodded. "I asked him if I should see a psychiatrist. He offered to refer me to one if I want, but since my amnesia is due to physical trauma, it's not likely a psychiatrist can help me."

"I'm so sorry. I know it's not what you wanted to hear, but the fact that your neurological exam was normal is excellent news. Was he encouraging about your memory coming back?"

"Kind of. He said he thought I would remember eventually. In the majority of cases people regain most of their memories. But there are some who never do." She looked at Sam. "It's my fault. I told him I wanted it straight and not to sugarcoat it."

"That doesn't surprise me. It's what I would have expected you to say. You're a very practical woman. Direct and straightforward."

"I've been thinking about calling Mitch. But he was so sure his brother could help me, I hate to tell him what the doctor said." Especially since Mitch was so damn determined that they couldn't get together until she got her memory back.

"Would it make you feel better to talk to him?"

She didn't need to think about that. "Yes."

"Then you should call him." She got up, walked over to the counter where she'd set the mail down. "Glenna, there's a package for you."

Glenna had been staring at the phone but at that she looked up. "For me?"

"Yes, from South America. It's postmarked San Rafael, Argentina."

San Rafael? It rang no bells, but that wasn't surprising. Not much did. "Who is it from?"

Sam squinted at the package. "Rosalie Torres. I can't read the return address. It's a PO box, but the number is illegible."

For a moment Glenna simply stared at Sam before accepting the small package, a padded envelope with Rosalie Torres's name on it. Rosalie Torres—the name on her phony passport. Addressed to Glenna Gallagher at the ranch's address in Marietta, Montana. What the hell?

"Is something wrong, Glenna? Something else, I mean? Is it the package? You look shaken up."

"I—I am."

"Do you remember Rosalie Torres?"

"Yes." She stared at the small package, wondering why she was so reluctant to open it.

"That's good, isn't it? Maybe your memories are coming back."

"No, that's not it."

"Who is she?"

Glenna looked up to meet Sam's concerned gaze. "Rosalie Torres is me. It's the name on my fake passport. I thought it was my real name until I met Mitch."

"Oh. That is a little…disconcerting."

Glenna's laugh held no humor. "Just a little."

"Are you going to open it?"

"I don't want to." She turned it over, weighed it in her hand. It was light. So light it could have been a letter. But obviously there was something else in there. "I have no idea why I feel that way."

"Then don't do it. Put it aside until you're ready to deal with it."

Glenna set it on the big table and looked at Sam. "Do you think I'm a coward?"

"Because you don't want to open that package? Of course not." She walked over and patted Glenna's arm. "You're in a terribly difficult situation, Glenna. Listen to your instincts. If you don't want to open this package, there's bound to be a reason, even if you don't consciously know what it is."

"I wish Mitch was here."

"So call him."

"I will."

Sam's phone rang just then. She answered with, "Dr. Striker. Oh, hi, Sean." Her expression changed to one of alarm. "How many people involved? How many are we getting?" She listened a moment then said, "I'll be right there."

She hung up. "There's been a multi-car pile-up on Highway 89. An eighteen-wheeler overturned and it sounds bad. Tell Dylan I had to go in. It's all hands on deck for this. At least until we know how many we have and how serious their injuries are."

Dylan walked in as Sam was rushing out the door. "Hey, I thought you were home for the afternoon?"

"Emergency. Glenna will tell you. Gotta go." She kissed him and ran out the door.

Dylan just shook his head. "Must be bad for her to leave like that on her afternoon off."

Glenna relayed what Sam had told her about the accident.

"Damn, I hope it's not as bad as it sounds. If it is, she'll pull an all-nighter on top of taking call last night."

"Does she have all-nighters a lot?"

"When she's on call. The hospital requires that there is a trauma surgeon at the hospital at all times. It's part of having a Level III Trauma Center. That doesn't mean it's busy every time she's on call, though. But trauma surgeons can and do get called in during emergencies. Like today."

"You're very proud of her and the work she does, aren't you?"

He smiled. "Yeah. Sam's amazing." Puzzled, he looked

around. "Where's Glory? She's usually got lunch fixings out by now."

"I haven't seen her since this morning before I left for my appointment. She said she was going to Livingston," Glenna added slowly. "Don't you take Highway 89 to get there?"

"Shit. Goddamn it." He pulled his phone out of his pocket and hit a couple of buttons. "No point calling Sam. She won't be there yet and when she does get there she'll go to surgery as quickly as possible. Pick up, damn it," he said into the phone.

"Sean, is Glory—" His worried expression turned to one of relief. "Thank God. Is Wyatt there? Okay, good. Has anyone called Bill? Good. I'll be there as soon as I can."

"Was Glory in the pile-up? What happened to her? Is she badly hurt?"

"Yes, she just came in. Sean says her arm is broken. Other than that, he thinks she'll be fine. Wyatt's there, so he can take care of her and decide what they need to do for her. Her husband Bill is on his way." He stood there a moment, then said, "I'm going down to the barn to tell the men what's going on and then I'll head out. It's not strictly necessary that I go, but, well, it's Glory. Do you want to come with me?"

On the one hand, she wanted to go. But on the other... "Are you sure I won't be in the way? I don't want to intrude."

Dylan gave her an exasperated look. "You're family.

There's no such thing as intruding when you're family." He thought about that a minute. "Well, in a case like this, anyway. I can think of several times my family has needed to butt out but they keep on 'helping'."

She smiled. "All right. Thanks."

Chapter Twenty

MITCH FOUND GLENNA in the hospital waiting room late that afternoon. She looked much as she had the first time he saw her, alone amidst a crowd of people. Only these people were her family. But then he noticed she wasn't as alone as he'd first thought. He could tell by her body language that she was more relaxed than he'd seen her yet around her family.

Austin had called him and told him about the wreck on Highway 89, the resulting pile-up, and that the Gallagher's housekeeper had been involved. He'd called the ranch and gotten the machine. As far as he knew, Glenna still had no phone. It annoyed him, because how hard was it to get a burner phone? It seemed like someone could have taken her to get one. Knowing Glenna, though, she wouldn't spend the money.

While he was standing there, Dylan's fiancée, Dr. Sam Striker, came into the waiting room and it looked like she was giving the family an update. Glenna, he was happy to see, had gathered round with the rest of them. She must have sensed he was there because she turned away from the group and looked right at him.

And smiled. Damn, she had a great smile. He walked to her and took her hands in his. "I heard about the wreck, and about your housekeeper. How is she?"

"Glory has a broken arm but she'll be okay. They don't think she'll need surgery, just a splint for now and possibly a cast after the swelling goes down. Her husband is here and he's going to take her home as soon as they release her."

"That's good. I called the ranch and didn't get you, so I thought I'd call your cell. Except you still don't have one, do you?"

"Yes, I do. Dylan bought me one yesterday. I was going to call to give you the number but then this happened," she said, motioning to include her family. "Speaking of calling you, will you take me home? There's something I want to show you."

"You sound upset. What is it?"

"A package came for me today. From Argentina."

"Villareal found you?" Damn. The last thing they needed.

"No, although I don't doubt he knows where I am by now, or at the least, suspects. No, this package is from Rosalie Torres."

What the hell? "Your alter ego? When did you mail it?"

"I can't read the date but the city is San Rafael. Obviously, I mailed it before my accident, and after I acquired the fake IDs. Or at least after I decided on that name. I haven't opened it yet. I know it's silly but I'm afraid of what I'll find." She shrugged. "It's just a package. How bad could it be?"

"How big is it?"

"It's a small padded envelope. It's very beat up, which makes sense considering I mailed it weeks ago and it's only now showed up in Marietta."

"It could be more evidence of the counterfeiting operation."

"If it is, I don't know what to do with it."

"Call the Secret Service."

"Oh, that's right. You told me that earlier. I still find it weird that the Secret Service handles counterfeiting."

"If it's evidence in a major counterfeiting operation, we definitely need to give it to the Secret Service. Otherwise we could turn it over to the local police, but in this case I think the Secret Service are the ones to contact. Or failing the Secret Service, the FBI. Can you leave now?"

"Yes. Let me tell Dylan. I came with him."

They left shortly after that. "You looked a little more at ease with your family," Mitch said, on the way to the Gallagher ranch.

"I am. Even though I still can't remember them, they're easy to get to know. Easy to talk to."

"That's great."

"It's nice. I had an interesting talk with Jack last night."

"Yeah? What about?"

"You, mostly."

"Do I need a flak jacket?"

"Of course not. Jack even said your actions spoke well of you. Personally, I'd call it your inaction."

"I'm lost." What in the hell was she talking about? Last time he'd seen Jack, which was also the first time he'd seen Jack, her oldest brother had looked like he wanted to rip Mitch apart with his bare hands.

"You don't know how to get to the ranch? How did you get there before?"

"Of course I know how to get to the ranch. What the hell are you talking about? My inaction?"

"Isn't it obvious?"

"Glenna," he said with a warning in his voice.

Which didn't appear to faze her, but at least she answered. "I told Jack that you say you don't want to take advantage of me, and I say that's bullshit."

"God help me." He turned off the highway onto the lane leading to the Gallagher ranch.

"Why? That's when Jack said it spoke well of you."

"And you said it was bullshit, but it's not, Glenna."

She shrugged. "Potato, po-taw-to."

Mitch gritted his teeth. Fortunately, they pulled up to the back door so he was spared saying anything in response to that deliberately provocative statement. *And she knows it, too,* he thought, glancing at her satisfied expression.

Glenna opened the kitchen door and walked in with him following. "I asked Dylan about a key but he said they never lock the door."

They heard barking and a medium-sized black dog burst into the kitchen with his ears perked up. When he saw Glenna he ran up to her, wiggling with delight. "Hi, Shadow. This is Mitch."

Mitch held out his hand for the dog to sniff.

"I forgot—have you met him before?" Glenna asked Mitch.

"No, he must have been outside." He patted his head and scratched behind his ears. "Good boy."

"He spends a lot of time with the other dogs and horses. But he sleeps with Dylan and Sam. From what I hear he's a hero."

"Really? What did he do?"

"He helped take down an arsonist. I think he bit him in the butt."

Mitch laughed. "That's one way to do it."

"It's quite a story. I'll tell you about it sometime."

"Where's this package?"

"I left it on the table." She picked up a small, padded mailer and passed it to him. "Like I told you, it's postmarked San Rafael, Argentina. Can you read the date?"

He squinted at it. "No, but if I had a magnifying glass I might be able to make it out." Mitch gave it back to her and waited for her to open it. After hesitating a long moment, she ripped it open, careful not to tear the date, and poured the contents into her hand. Something small, wrapped in bubble wrap, sat on her palm. She peeled away the wrap to reveal a small, black jump drive.

"Any bets on what this is?" Glenna asked.

"No bets. More of a sure thing. Something that ties the Villareals to the counterfeiting operation would give them a great reason to come after you."

"If that's true, I wonder why I didn't keep it with the phony bills?"

"You probably thought it safer to split up the evidence. The fact that you mailed it to yourself here at the ranch almost certainly means you intended to come here."

"Until I got derailed by a pesky old bus accident. I'm sure someone around here has a computer. We can look at it."

"I'm sure they do, but I'd rather pull it up on my computer."

"All right. Let me leave a note and I'll be ready."

MITCH TOOK GLENNA back to his hotel room. He knew she wouldn't be left behind, so he didn't even try. He needed to have this information, whatever it was, on his computer. Most of all, he wanted to give all of the information to someone in the government. He figured the less time he or Glenna had it, the better it would be for them. And if it was evidence, the faster the authorities could bust that counterfeiting operation.

It was also possible that seeing what was on the jump drive would trigger Glenna's memory. Mitch wasn't holding out a lot of hope for that. After all, nothing else had brought back her memories.

But he wasn't sure how much longer he could hold out before he broke down and made love with Glenna regardless of all the reasons why they shouldn't. Good reasons, which would make a difference if he weren't in love with her.

In love? What? He couldn't be in love with her. He'd been cured of that when he was twenty years old. Or so he'd thought. But if he wasn't in love with Glenna, then what the hell was wrong with him?

And what about her? She still had no memory of her life before the accident. If it turned out she really was married, she'd said she'd get a divorce. He'd bet his last dime the man had driven her to flee, away from him and the ranch she'd called home. Mitch couldn't see her staying with him, especially if the Villareals proved to be key in a counterfeiting operation.

Was it fair to Glenna to have sex with her when she still had amnesia? What if, as she feared, her memory never came back? What were they supposed to do then?

They weren't talking about a serious relationship. Or were they? God knows, Glenna was different from any other woman he'd ever known. Maybe it wouldn't work out between them, but why deny them the chance to try?

You are so damn hopeless. You're just trying to justify taking her to bed, asshole.

I don't need to justify it. She wants it too. It's not like I have to talk her into something she doesn't want to do.

Rationalization. You're good at that.

Shut up.

"Wow," Glenna said when they walked into the Graff lobby. "This is beautiful."

"It's nice."

"Nice? That's all you can say?" She waved a hand at the elegant lobby, complete with dark-beamed high ceilings, a huge chandelier and seating areas scattered throughout.

"No. The food is good too. Speaking of food, let's order room service. I'm betting you haven't had dinner and I'm hungry."

"That's fine," she said, still looking around. "Are the rooms decorated like this too?"

Mitch shrugged. "Kind of, I guess. You'll see for yourself. It's a nice room. Big and spacious, nothing too flashy. Looks kind of old-fashioned."

Glenna shook her head and followed him into the elevator.

When they walked into his room Mitch decided to order food first, since he wasn't sure how long it would take. "Here, see what you want." He handed her the menu.

"The club sandwich looks good. What are you getting?"

"Their hamburgers are great."

"I haven't had a hamburger since—" She broke off, then laughed. "I have no idea when I last ate a hamburger. I'd like one too."

Mitch ordered for them then went to the small wooden writing desk where his laptop sat. Glenna explored the room while he waited for the computer to boot up. "Want me to pull up a chair for you?" he asked her.

"No, I'll just stand behind you. I doubt it will take that long unless there's a ton of stuff on it. Besides, we really don't know what is on the drive. It might not even be important."

"Which is why you mailed it to your real self in the US from your fake self in Argentina," he countered skeptically.

She scowled at him. He plugged in the small drive and pulled up the files. Spreadsheets. A lot of them, it looked like. Mitch clicked on one of the spreadsheets at random. "People in the organization, possibly. Or mules. They have to distribute the money somehow." He opened another and scrolled down. "Cost of various supplies. Paper, Venezuelan notes, ink, glue, flour… Glue and flour? I'm not sure what those are about."

He opened yet another. "This is a detailed list of when and what supplies were ordered, when they came in, how much was wasted. You downloaded the mother lode of incriminating documents here. Where do you suppose you found this information?" She didn't answer.

He turned around to look at her. Glenna had turned

sheet-white and was hanging on to the back of his chair, white-knuckled. He jumped up and grabbed her, afraid she was going to pass out. "What's wrong? Did you remember something?"

"My head... I can't... Oh, God." She covered her eyes with her hands, as if to block out whatever vision she saw.

"Come on," he said, half-carrying her to the couch. "Sit down and put your head between your legs."

She did as he instructed. Mitch watched her anxiously, wondering if he should call a doctor. Hell, she had three brothers and a soon-to-be sister-in-law who were doctors. He took his phone out of his pocket to call them.

Glenna raised her head. "Who are you calling?"

She looked better. Marginally. "You scared the shit out of me. I'm calling your family. They're doctors. They can decide if you need to go to the hospital."

"Don't call them. Please. I'm all right now."

He reserved judgment on that but she was looking better by the moment. He turned off his phone and set it on the desk. Then he ejected the drive before turning back to Glenna. "Can you tell me what happened?"

"I—I don't know. It was the strangest thing." She rubbed her temples. "I had a flash of something. A computer. I was downloading files. I was nervous...hoping he wouldn't come in."

"Who is he?"

"I don't know. When I tried to concentrate, to remember what I'd seen more clearly, I thought my head would explode."

Was she starting to get her memory back? It sure as shit sounded like it. "Don't force it, then. You're not ready to remember all of it—whatever this is." The fact that it made her sick to try to remember didn't bode well, however. "I'll see about contacting the Secret Service or the FBI in the morning. There's a satellite FBI office in Bozeman. I'm sure they'll want to talk to you."

"That will do a lot of good. Can't you email the files?

"I could, but I'd rather give the drive to a person. The actual jump drive might tell them something we miss."

"This must be why those men were after me. You were right. The Villareals must have sent them to get the drive back. I wonder how they knew I had it?"

"We may never know the answer to that." He looked at her critically. "You look better, but damn, don't do that again."

"It didn't feel too good from where I'm sitting, either. But I'm fine now. As long as I don't think about those spreadsheets."

Someone knocked on the door. "Room Service."

Mitch let the waiter in, had him put the tray on the coffee table and signed his name to the bill. "When did you eat last?"

"Breakfast."

"This should make you feel better. No wonder you almost fainted."

She lifted her nose in the air. "I didn't almost faint. I was simply unwell for a minute."

"Potato, po-taw-to."

That drew a smile from her. "Touché." She started on her hamburger. "This is really good. I must like hamburgers."

They ate mostly in silence, but it was companionable not awkward.

"You were right," Glenna said after demolishing almost everything on her plate. "I feel better now. Could I use your restroom?"

"Of course." She took her purse with her and disappeared into his bathroom. Mitch wasn't sure why he thought Glenna was up to something but he did.

Chapter Twenty-One

GLENNA SHUT THE bathroom door and looked in the mirror. Not awful, but she'd sure as hell looked better. Sam had lent her a purse, a large brown bag that Glenna dumped everything from her backpack into, except for her clothes.

The first thing she did was to take the band out of her hair and brush it. Then she used some of Mitch's toothpaste to brush her teeth with her finger. She dug around for her small stash of makeup, set it on the counter and went to work. A little eye makeup, a bit of lipstick, and she was done. *That's as good as it's going to get.*

There wasn't a whole lot she could do about her clothes. When she'd left for the hospital, she'd been wearing jeans and a button-down white cotton shirt over a white sleeveless T-shirt with a built-in bra. She took off the top shirt and stuffed it in her bag. Better. Not great but it would have to do.

It was pretty freaking obvious that if she wanted Mitch, she was going to have to take matters into her own hands. If he turned her down this time... Best not think about that. She knew he wanted her. She could not be so deluded that she thought he wanted her when he didn't.

You have amnesia, girl. Of course you could be deluded.

Bending over, she fluffed her hair, stood up and looked in the mirror one last time. Then she left her bag on the counter, opened the door and stepped out.

Mitch sat on the couch, head down as he fiddled with his phone. Without looking up he asked, "Are you ready for me to take you home?"

"No."

He looked at her then. His eyes widened, then narrowed. "What are you doing, Glenna?"

She walked over to stand in front of him. "You're a smart guy. I think you can figure that out." Apparently, she'd robbed him of speech. She sat in his lap and looped her arms around his neck. "Tell me you don't want me. That's all you have to do and I'll stop throwing myself at you."

For a long moment he simply looked at her. Finally, he said, "I can't," and crushed his mouth to hers.

She was drowning in his kiss. In the smell of him, the taste of him, the feel of that rock-solid body next to hers. His kiss was not sweet, or gentle, or easy. It was steaming hot and full of purpose. This kiss said he wanted her and this time there would be no holding back, no hesitation, no retreat.

He slipped his hand beneath her shirt to fondle her breasts. She sucked in a breath, her nipples tightening at the warmth of his hand on her bare skin. He helped her turn to straddle him, pushed up her shirt and stripped it off. One hand on her breasts, the other caressing her butt, pressing her sex against his, his lips on hers, his tongue in her mouth tasting her, seducing her.

Mitch stood and she wrapped herself around him, kissing him as he walked them both toward the bed. Glenna landed on her back, her legs open to welcome him.

"You have no idea how long I've wanted to do this," Mitch said roughly, lying down beside her.

"As long as I've wanted you to. Almost from the first."

"Yes. From the first moment I laid eyes on you." He kissed her again, sliding his tongue inside her mouth, teasing, testing, taunting. Breaking for air, she tugged at his T-shirt. "Take this off."

"Gladly." He rolled off of her and stood, yanking his shirt off before looking down at her, smiling. "Damn, Glenna, you're beautiful."

She held out a hand. "So are you."

He shook his head, still smiling.

"I don't suppose you have a condom?"

His smile widened. "I suppose I do." He stepped into the bathroom.

Glenna got up, unbuttoned and unzipped her jeans and stripped them off, along with her socks. Mitch came up behind her, moved her hair aside to kiss her neck and shoulder. After tossing a condom packet on the bed, he covered her breasts with his hands and she could feel his erection pressing against her. He turned her around, pushed her onto the bed and came down beside her.

He caressed her breasts, tugging on the nipples gently, teasing them to hard points. His hands played with her while he kissed and sucked each breast. His fingers slid inside her and out, then did it again, and again teasing her to madness. Her back arched, her hips bucked, each movement of his fingers bringing her closer to the edge.

She slid her hand down and stroked his shaft. He was hard and getting harder. She wanted him inside her, now. Pushing him onto his back, she picked up the condom, tore open the packet and reached for him.

He laughed and said, "Better let me. I told you, it's been a long time." He put it on, then he rolled on top of her, spreading her legs, his cock, warm and hard, pressed against her, nudging at her opening. He kissed her and began to enter her, slowly. She raised her hips and met him, tightening her muscles as he plunged into her until he was seated deep inside. She moaned and twisted restlessly.

"Too much?" he asked hoarsely.

"No, just right," she said pressing her hips upward.

He drove into her then, pulling out and sinking back in, faster and faster and she spiraled higher and higher, exploding at the peak. Mitch thrust into her a final time, a husky groan, and then moaned her name as he came.

After a while he disappeared into the bathroom. A moment later, he returned and pulled her into his arms, her cheek lying against his chest.

"Are you sorry?" she asked.

His chuckle rumbled against her ear. "Do I look sorry?"

She drew back and looked at him, traced a finger over his lips. "No, you look satisfied."

"I am. For now," he added, his voice dropping.

Just that implication made her stomach flutter and the ache between her legs intensify.

When he continued talking it made her ache even more. "Later, if it's okay with you, I'm going to explore all those places I missed the first time."

"Are you? I think I'd like that." She kissed him again and said, "Once you make up your mind, you put your whole self into it, don't you?"

"I'm a very thorough person."

"Why did you resist so long?"

"So long?" He smiled. "We've only known each other for a little over a week."

"Oh, yeah. Well, it seems like I've known you forever."

"That's because I'm the only person you do know."

"I don't think that's the reason. Or not all of it, anyway." And she was about to get into a spot where she didn't think Mitch wanted to go, so she changed the subject. "I'm glad you had condoms. In Santiago, when you said you hadn't been with anyone in a long time, I thought you wouldn't have any."

"I didn't. Then. I bought them the day we got to Marietta. After you kissed me and announced to your brothers that we were going to get together."

"Really? You said nothing was going to happen."

"Yeah, I know. I was just fooling myself. But I didn't trust myself around you. For obvious reasons since here we are in bed together."

"There's no place I'd rather be." If only they could stay here, where she could be completely herself—whoever that was—and not worry about disappointing anyone. Not think about a family she wanted to remember, yet couldn't. Not worry about spreadsheets and counterfeit money and bad guys coming after her.

Where she could be with Mitch and love him and not think about anything else.

GLENNA CALLED HER soon-to-be sister-in-law, Sam, and told her she wouldn't be home that night. Mitch didn't blame her for choosing to tell Sam rather than Dylan. He didn't at all look forward to her brothers' reactions to the news that their amnesiac sister was getting it on with the PI who'd found her.

She hung up, turned her phone to silent, and put it on the bedside table.

"Everything okay?"

Glenna smiled. "Everything is great. She told me to have

fun."

"Somehow I don't think that will be Dylan's reaction."

"Dylan's pretty reasonable. They all are, really. They know I'm going to do what I want and they have no say in it. Well, other than owing them a ton of money."

"Which I'm sure they're demanding payment of right away."

She frowned. "You know they're not. But Dylan did say he'd hire me to help with the horses. Once he figured out I was intent on getting a paying job, and repaying what they spent on me, he said he'd hire me at the going rate."

"That's great. When do you start?" It didn't surprise him that Glenna was determined to pay back her family. Just another indication that she wasn't a taker. She stood firmly on her own, paid her own way, and didn't like to be beholden to anyone, not even family.

"I thought I'd ask him if he wants me to start work tomorrow. Maybe after we take the jump drive to the authorities."

She wore one of his button-down shirts with the top two buttons undone and her breasts peeking out whenever she moved. Her legs were long, bare and silky soft below the hem of the shirt. Why was it that a woman could make a man's shirt look so damn sexy?

Boobs, for one thing.

Legs, for another.

"What are you staring at?"

Mitch reached out and ran his finger down the opening of his shirt. "You, what else?" He slipped his hand inside to cover her breast, cup it, use his thumb to tease her nipple to attention.

Glenna dropped her head back and closed her eyes, giving a tiny moan of pleasure. He kissed her jaw, the curve of her neck, the hollow at the base of her throat. Reached beneath the shirt to strip off her panties. He spared a moment to wonder why she'd put them back on when she knew he would only remove them again. He slipped his hands beneath the panties and drew them slowly down her legs, following the progress with his lips. Flung the panties aside and kissed his way back up her legs.

Glenna hadn't been idle. While he was working his way up her beautiful legs, she unbuttoned the shirt and wiggled out of it. "Now?" she asked, her voice a low, sexy timbre.

He looked at her, smiled and shook his head. "Not yet. I made a promise to explore everything I missed the first time around and I haven't even gotten started."

"When you put it that way…"

SINCE THERE WASN'T a Secret Service office anywhere remotely close, Glenna and Mitch wound up taking the jump drive to the FBI satellite field office in Bozeman. It occupied their entire morning but Glenna thought it was worth it to be able to hand over that evidence and have the whole question of counterfeiting be somebody else's problem.

When they returned to the ranch, Glenna asked Mitch to stay for a while and meet the horses and see Dylan's operation. Her brother was doing really well breeding his horses. Most of his horses were Norwegian Fjords. According to Dylan, they'd had quarter horses when they were growing up. Dylan had raised them too, but then he'd seen the Norwegian Fjords and fallen in love with them, and now he'd been raising them for a number of years.

Dylan and Glenna had agreed on a wage the day before. "Do you need an advance on your wages?" Dylan asked her when he met her and Mitch down at the barn. "You're bound to need some money."

"No, I'm fine." She wasn't really, but she could make do until payday. "Dylan, we haven't discussed how much you should take out of my paycheck to settle my debt."

"That's because I'm not taking your money."

"We've talked about this before, Dylan."

"And I told you then I didn't want your money."

"Fine, then you'll pay me and I'll immediately turn around and give some of it to you. Which seems like a complete waste of time."

"Can you talk some sense into her?" Dylan asked Mitch.

"Not if she's made up her mind. Looks like she has. You might as well do what she asks."

Dylan frowned at her. "You're going to pay us back, even

though we don't want it, aren't you? Damn, Glenna, you are one determined woman."

You are a very determined woman.

That voice. She knew that voice. She shuddered as the memories cascaded through her mind.

She was Volcán's last chance. A magnificent Criollo stallion, coal black with white socks and a white stripe on his nose, Volcán was slated to be sold if she couldn't tame him.

But damn, the gorgeous animal was almost as stubborn as she was. Almost. She was determined to ride him; he was equally determined that she wouldn't stay on longer than a few seconds. She mounted him. He bucked her off. She climbed back on. He threw her again. She climbed back on again. Over and over until she and Volcán came to an understanding. She rode him long enough to cement the lesson, then she dismounted and fed him a sugar cube. She led him into the barn to cool him down. Took off his saddle and the blanket and grabbed a brush.

Glenna patted his cheek and fed him another sugar cube and began brushing him. "There, Volcán, that wasn't so bad, was it?" No, she was the one who would ache for days.

"*You are a very determined woman.*"

Startled, Glenna realized the man she'd thought was one of the ranch hands watching her was actually Rolando Villareal, only son of her boss, Jorge Villareal. She'd seen him before, of course, but always at a distance. Rolando didn't spend a lot of time at the ranch and never had in the years that she had worked there. Rumor had it he preferred a more cosmopolitan existence. He'd come home occasionally, but always left after a short time. A couple of days at most.

Rolando Villareal was heir to an empire. When his father had taken ill a couple of weeks before, Rolando had come home to take over the family business—running the enormous ranch. The cattle business had been going well until a couple of months before. It started faltering first, for no discernable reason. Then the animals fell prey to a disease that in the end wiped out three-quarters of the herd.

At his father's request, so she'd heard, Rolando came home to save the family ranch. She didn't know exactly what he'd been doing since he arrived home, but he hadn't concerned himself with the part Glenna managed—the cattle business. Maybe he'd come to discuss it with her. Or fire her. Probably fire her, even though she'd come to the conclusion that Jorge had been siphoning off money, though she didn't know why.

At any rate, here was Rolando, watching Glenna get her butt kicked by an ornery horse. At least she'd won out in the end. It would have been humiliating if she'd had to give up. She wished she didn't look as bedraggled as she felt, but she didn't need a mirror to know that she did.

"Forgive me," Rolando said, adding a winsome smile, "but aren't you the ranch cattle manager? Is breaking horses one of your duties?"

"Not normally. But I have a—a knack for getting into the heads of the really stubborn ones."

That was the beginning of what developed into a passionate affair. Far from firing her, according to Rolando, he fell in love with her in the moment he saw her.

Later, Glenna discovered Rolando didn't admire her determination. He wanted to destroy it. Wanted her to be his, under his thumb, under his control. Much of the pleasure he took was in turning a strong, independent woman into his willing slave, dependent on him for the very food she ate.

But she saw none of that. At first. She saw the illusion Rolando presented. The handsome, suave and charming playboy who finally met his match and wanted to commit to her. Yet something held her back.

Honestly, she'd thought once they slept together Rolando would lose interest. But he didn't. Whether it was because he was stuck at the ranch for the foreseeable future, or because he really had feelings for her, she couldn't be sure.

He said he loved her. Wanted to marry her. Wanted her to bear his children. His children...

When she came back to herself, Mitch was sitting on the ground, holding her, and both he and Dylan were looking at her anxiously.

"Good God, Glenna, what happened?" Mitch asked. "You turned white as snow and damn near passed out."

"You'd have hit the ground if Mitch hadn't caught you," Dylan added. "Are you sick?"

Her ability to breathe was slowly returning. "Not—not physically. I remembered. Oh, God, I remembered."

"What did you remember, Glenna?" Mitch asked. His tone was gentle and soothing. "Just breathe. Take a few breaths and tell us when you're ready."

Glenna clutched Mitch's hand. "Rolando. I remembered

the first time I met him." She went on to tell them about *Volcán* and the rest of her flashback. And about her certainty that at the least, she'd been involved with Rolando.

"Did you marry him?" Dylan asked.

"I don't think so. But he wanted me to. I don't know why I held back. Maybe I sensed something was off about him. Maybe I knew something about the counterfeiting by then. Or maybe I just wasn't ready to commit to him." She spread her hands in a gesture of futility. "But if I did marry him, it wasn't part of what I remembered."

"Your memory is coming back, though," Mitch said. "That's a good thing."

"Is it? I'm not so sure," she said slowly.

"Why?" Dylan asked.

"There's something there, in the back of my mind. Just out of reach." She let go of Mitch's hand and rubbed her temples. "Whenever I think about it, or try to remember it, a door slams shut in my mind and all I know is that I'm scared. Scared to death."

"Of Rolando?" Mitch asked.

Glenna shook her head. "I don't know. But who or what else would it be?"

Chapter Twenty-Two

THEY WENT UP to the house after that, both men insisting Glenna needed to take a break and have a cup of coffee or at least some water. Glory was there, broken arm and all.

"What in the hell are you doing here?" Dylan asked Glory.

"I work here."

"Not for at least a week, you don't. Shit, Glory, you're still in a splint. You don't even have a cast yet."

"Don't think you can tell me what to do, Dylan Gallagher. Why, there's no telling what the kitchen will look like if I leave you to your own devices for that long."

"You're supposed to be taking it easy. We don't need you. We'll survive without your cooking for a few more days."

"Ha! No, you can't. And don't think you're going to make Sam do all the cooking. She's got her hands full with the hospital."

"I know that. We'll scrounge until you get back. Now go

on home."

"I can cook until you come back," Glenna offered.

"Since when?" Glory asked.

Dylan choked off a laugh.

"What? I can cook," she said, looking from one to the other. "Can't I?" she asked Mitch.

"Don't look at me," Mitch said. "Cooking hasn't been high on our list of priorities."

"That's sweet of you," Glory said. "But you never could cook a lick. Unless you've changed."

"Just because I burned a few cookies a time or two—" Glenna began.

"A few cookies?" Dylan laughed so hard he had to hold his sides.

Glory laughed too. "Oh, honey, you burned everything you ever touched."

Insulted, Glenna put her hands on her hips and glared at both of them. "No, I didn't. I only burned the cookies once and that was Dylan's fault for distracting—" She stopped mid-sentence. "I was fourteen," she said slowly. "Dylan was thirteen and I was making slice-and-bake cookies to take to school. He wanted me to come look at one of the horses. So I did and I...I forgot about the cookies."

"And started a fire in my oven," Glory said.

"You were so mad you wouldn't let me near the oven for months."

"That's right. And the next time I did, you burned a casserole we were having for dinner."

"I remember," she said, staring at the two of them. "I remember you," she said to Dylan and hugged him. Turning to Glory, she threw her arms around her, but carefully. "And you." She let go and hugged Dylan again. "I remember all of you. Jack, Sean, and Wyatt, too. Oh, my God, I remember all of you."

Dylan's grin was a mile wide. "Looks like you do. About time."

Mitch was grinning too. "Congratulations. You broke the jam."

"Some of it. I'm still hazy on the details of what happened in Argentina. But I remember everything about home." She frowned and added, "Including why I left. We were right. Dad and I had a huge fight. I told him I was going to be a rancher and he laughed at me. When he realized I was serious, he told me I never would be. But I could be a rancher's wife. That's when he decided on the terms of his stupid will."

"Exactly what we suspected," Dylan said.

They called the rest of the family to tell them about Glenna's breakthrough and arranged to all get together the following night to celebrate her recovery.

"YOU LOOK HAPPY," Mitch said when they got back to the hotel.

"That's because I am. I have my family back. Even though I hadn't seen them in a long time it has always helped to know they were there. It's very disconcerting to know you have a family and not remember anything about them."

"I'm sure it is."

"But…" she said, beginning to unbutton her shirt, "that's not what I want to talk about right now."

Mitch sat on the bed and took off his boots and socks. "No? What do you want to talk about?"

"Silly man," she said, climbing onto his lap and straddling him, her shirt hanging open. "I don't want to talk at all." She wound her arms around his neck and kissed him.

Hot honey. That's what she tasted like. As potent as a straight shot of bourbon, burning its way to his gut.

Clothes went flying. He stripped off her shirt and bra. She pushed his shirt up so he could yank it off over his head. She kissed him again, bare breasts to his bare chest, and rocked her sex against his.

Mitch groaned, going from half-aroused to fully erect in a heartbeat. "Whoa, Tiger. Slow down," he managed to get out between hot, open-mouthed kisses.

"I don't want to slow down." She climbed off his lap, stripped off her jeans and panties, then stood in front of him. Naked. Tempting. Beautiful.

He took a long look at her from top to bottom. She reached for his jeans, rubbed her hand up and down his cock.

He sucked in a breath. "Forget slow." He stood and pushed jeans and boxers off in one move, then sat and reached for her.

Glenna grabbed a condom and rolled it down his length, excruciatingly slowly. Then she pushed him onto his back, poised herself over him and sank down on him until his cock was buried deep inside her. She rode them both to a screaming climax that seemed to last forever, then collapsed in a boneless heap on top of him.

Later, they lay on the bed together, his arm around her, her head on his chest, her hair streaming over her shoulders and his chest in a gorgeous red cloud.

"What are you thinking about?" she asked softly.

Glenna didn't know it but that was a loaded question. Because for the first time since his ill-considered and ill-fated marriage he was thinking about…settling down?

Not exactly. You're thinking about what you're going to have to do to keep Glenna. Because you're not done with her. Hell, you don't want to be done with her. Ever.

Damn, man, yesterday was the first time you had sex with her and now you're ready to change your whole life for her?

Not just sex. The best sex of my life.

You've been through that before.

No. Because this time I'm in love. Totally crazy in love with Glenna.

The short answer was yes.

"Mitch?"

It's too soon, dumbass. Way too soon. Which he knew, but he ignored his common sense. He tugged gently on her hair until her head tilted back and she was looking into his eyes. "I'm in love with you, Glenna."

Her eyes widened and then she smiled. A smile of pure, joyous sunshine. "That's handy. Because I'm in love with you."

FEELING ENCOURAGED FOR the first time, Glenna left Dr. Hardeman's office. All of her tests had come back negative, which the doctor had expected, but it was still a relief to hear. Dr. Hardeman thought that her recent breakthroughs were a very good sign that most of her memory would return, but of course, he couldn't predict when that would happen.

Mitch had come with her, but he'd said he had something to handle while she saw his brother.

Poised to open the truck's door, a hand covered hers, and a familiar voice said, "Surprised to see me, *querida?*"

She turned and looked into Rolando Villareal's eyes. Cold steel jabbed into her neck, hot breath in her ear, his hand gripping hers painfully. "*¿Dondé esta mi hijo?*"

Where is my son? Clearly, Rolando had known or figured out she'd been pregnant when she left. But just as obviously, he didn't know about the accident and the miscarriage.

He jabbed the gun hard against her neck and asked again. "What have you done with my son, *puta*?" A curtain lifted and the scene played out her mind.

Glenna was late meeting Valencia. She'd thrown together a few clothes, a few toiletries, her IDs and as much real cash as she could find, which was damn little. Then she'd put the stack of fake currency and the jump drive in a plastic bag and tossed it in her backpack. Knowing Rolando would trace her, she'd left her phone out in a far pasture. It wouldn't fool him for long, but it was the best she could do.

She'd been to the stable earlier to tell Volcán goodbye. Made that much harder by not being able to let anyone know that's what she was really doing. She entered the stable, expecting to find Valencia, wondering what had kept her, but there was no sign of her.

Moaning. She heard moaning coming from one of the stalls, and it wasn't a horse. Her stomach jittered as she opened the door and looked inside. "Valencia! Oh, my God, Valencia!"

Her friend lay on the straw in the empty stall. Her blood ran freely from between her fingers as she pressed her hands against her stomach. Glenna ran to her and cradled Valencia in her arms. She felt for her pulse and sagged with relief that she found it. "Thank God. Valencia, look at me."

Her relief was short-lived.

Valencia opened her eyes. "Go. You must go. Rolando knows you're pregnant."

"Did Rolando do this to you?"

"Sí. The money...he knows you...found the building. I'm

sorry, so sorry."

Tears streamed down Glenna's cheeks. "I'm not leaving you. We have to get you to a hospital."

"No, chica, it's no use. I'm...dying." She moved her hands away so Glenna could see the blood spilling rapidly. "I hoped...you'd find me...before he... Get out. Leave now, before...he comes back. Save yourself...and your child."

Valencia spoke with an effort, her sentences halting, pausing to gather her strength. Watching the blood drain out of her, Glenna feared she was right. "Come with me. I'll take you to a hospital. I'll take one of the cars."

"No. Too late. Run."

Moments later Valencia was gone.

The memories formed a kaleidoscope in her mind. Each one flashing a snapshot and fading into the next. Rolando...Valencia...Volcán...Rolando... All with a healthy dose of fear growing stronger with each memory. With a jolt, she came back to the present. "Oh, my God. I remember."

"What do you remember, *querida*?"

His voice was smooth, silky, and evil. Valencia. Rolando had shot her in cold blood. And if Glenna told him she'd lost his child, he'd kill her too.

She turned to face him, ignoring the gun he held. "If you kill me you'll never find your son."

His face darkened with fury. "You have no right. No right to keep him from me."

"I have every right to keep him safe."

"Keep him safe? My men say they never saw him. You

sent him away because you couldn't be bothered."

"I sent him away to keep him safe." *Keep him talking. Keep him busy long enough for Mitch to show up.*

And then what?

Never mind that. Just talk.

"Safe from what?"

"From you."

His stunned silence told her she'd managed to shock him. "Why would you want to protect my son from me—his father?"

"Gee, I don't know, Rolando," she said, dripping sarcasm. "Perhaps because I don't want him to grow up to be a criminal." Or a murderer, but she didn't add that. Not yet.

Out of the corner of her eye, she saw Mitch coming. Relief was followed quickly by fear. For Mitch. What was to stop Rolando from simply turning the gun on Mitch before Mitch could do anything to stop him?

Chapter Twenty-Three

ONCE MITCH HAD made the decision to stay in Marietta, the rest was easy. He didn't need to close down his PI practice right away, or even at all, if he didn't want to. But if he intended to make Marietta his home base and not travel constantly he needed to either change his base of operations and change his focus or look for a different job. So while Glenna was seeing his brother, Mitch had an informal interview with hospital security. Unfortunately, the job didn't sound like anything he would be happy doing. But hell, he'd only just started thinking about it, and he wasn't on a timetable.

Not to mention, although she'd admitted she loved him, he had no idea what Glenna wanted to do. Except now that she'd remembered her family he had a feeling she'd want to stay in Marietta. At least for a while.

As he walked out in the parking lot and headed to the truck, he saw Glenna talking to a tall, dark-haired man. Inside of a minute Mitch realized it was Villareal. And he held a fucking gun on her. Mitch ducked behind the adjacent row of cars, trusting that Glenna had seen him and that she'd keep Villareal distracted long enough for Mitch to get the jump on him.

"You know nothing," Villareal snapped. "I'm no criminal."

"Oh, really? I suppose that counterfeiting ring operating from your ranch has nothing to do with you? You know the FBI now has the information I downloaded from your computer, don't you?"

"Bitch," he snarled, furiously. "You'll pay for that."

"No, I don't think I will. Unless you kill me right now, and you won't do that because you want your son."

"Why don't I kill you and get the information from your family?"

She laughed. "I'd like to see you try. They don't even know I was ever pregnant, much less that I have a child or where I've sent him."

Villareal stepped forward. Glenna stepped forward at the same time, grabbed his gun hand, and yanked it toward her, bending back his wrist and sliding the gun out of his hand, exactly like Mitch had taught her. Before Villareal could react, Mitch jumped him and took him to the ground. Villareal wasn't nearly as easy to subdue as his thugs had been and he landed a few good blows before Mitch finally pinned him down.

Mitch glanced at Glenna and smiled. "I was going to ask if you were all right, but I can see you are." She held the gun unwaveringly pointed at Villareal.

"Yes, but I'm glad you're here."

Villareal cursed in Spanish. Mitch and Glenna spoke at the same time. "¡*Cállate, pendejo!*"

"Call the cops, Glenna."

"My hands are full right now."

"I'll take the gun." He got up, snarling at Villareal when he moved. "Stay right there. Better yet, don't, and give me an excuse to shoot you."

Not too much later, the Marietta cops came to take Villareal and hold him for the Feds. Before they led him away, Glenna asked them to wait a minute.

"Rolando." The look the man gave her, unsurprisingly, was laced with hatred. "There is no child."

"You lie."

"No, I had a miscarriage. I was in a bus accident and lost the baby. So all this was for nothing. Except to put you in an excellent place to get caught," she added. "And by the way, I also told them about the murder you committed. Murder and counterfeiting should put you away for a long time."

Mitch wondered if the man might actually burst a blood vessel, but beyond pointless cursing there wasn't anything he could do stuck between two cops with his hands cuffed behind him.

"Murder?" Mitch asked Glenna when they'd gone.

"Yes. Rolando murdered my friend, Valencia. That's why I was running and why I was so afraid. Except I didn't remember until I heard Rolando's voice. I'd blocked it out. Her eyes welled with tears. "He shot her, Mitch. In cold blood."

Mitch pulled her into his arms. "He'll pay for it now. Thanks to you."

"And you," she said.

ALMOST TWO WEEKS later Glenna and Mitch sat with the entire Gallagher clan in the living room of the farmhouse.

"I now pronounce you husband and wife," the preacher said. "Kiss your bride, Dylan."

A little surprised to find herself teary, Glenna watched Dylan and Samantha's first kiss as husband and wife. "They look so happy," she said to Mitch with a sigh. "I think they're good for each other."

"The rest of your family seems happy too," Mitch said.

In the weeks since she'd been back, and especially since she'd regained her memory, Glenna had spent a lot of time with her family. Getting to know her brothers again, along with their wives and kids, had truly made Glenna feel like a part of the family. Jack was still the only one with kids, although Wyatt's wife, Mia, was due in a couple of months. And Sean and Honey had announced they were having a baby just the day before.

Jack and Maya had brought their new dog, Rambo, along, a rescue Carmen and Gina had found at school and brought home. While he'd been banished to the kitchen during the ceremony, they'd let him out as soon as it was over. Dylan and Sam's dog, Shadow, had been a part of the ceremony. Dylan had been very close-mouthed and mysterious about who would be his best man. He didn't ask any of his brothers and speculation about who it would be had been rampant.

"I don't think I've ever seen a dog be the best man before," Glenna said. "But Shadow managed it beautifully." She added, watching the two dogs playing with each other, "Sam told me she was just glad Dylan hadn't wanted his stallion, Trouble, to do the honors."

"That would've been interesting," Mitch said.

"Very. But they decided Trouble was still too easily spooked." She laughed. "Too bad. I would have paid to see it."

Jack came over and talked about the wedding a bit before saying, "As your oldest brother, I've been elected to ask you something."

"Well, that sounds ominous. What?"

"Are you two planning to get married before your birthday at the end of next month?"

Mitch choked off a laugh while Glenna glared at Jack. "We haven't discussed marriage, Mr.—I mean Dr. Nosy. Tell everyone to butt out of my business."

Not chastened at all, Jack responded, "We thought you might need to be reminded that if you get married before your next birthday, we can take care of the conditions of the will and give you your share."

He looked at Mitch and said, "We've tried to give Glenna her rightful portion of the ranch anyway, but she's too damned stubborn to accept."

"She's a little hardheaded," Mitch agreed. "But we'll talk about it and get back with you."

"Do that," Jack said. "And Mitch?" Mitch looked at him. "Good luck."

"Ignore him," Glenna began. "I don't know why he thinks—"

"I think we should," Mitch interrupted.

"That's what I said. We should ignore him."

"Not ignore him. We should get married."

Glenna stared at him, certain she hadn't heard him correctly. "What did you say?"

"I said we should get married. But that's wrong."

"Oh." *Gee, thanks. I'd just as soon you hadn't told me that.*

"Come with me." Mitch grabbed her hand and pulled her along with him.

"Where are we—"

He opened the library door, pulled Glenna inside and backed her up against the door. Hands on either side of her face, he looked down at her with a smile.

"Trying to decide whether to kiss me or strangle me?" Glenna asked.

"No. I know exactly what I want to do with you."

The way he looked at her made her heart slam against her chest. "Wh—what?" she stuttered.

"Marry me, Glenna."

"I thought you weren't ever getting married again."

"I changed my mind. I hadn't met you when I said that."

"I don't want you to feel pressured to marry me. I'm fine with just being with you."

Mitch bent his head down and kissed her. She started to speak and he kissed her again. "You know me better than that. Do you really think I'd ask you to marry me because I felt pressured?"

She gazed into his eyes. "No."

"I love you. Say you'll marry me, Glenna."

"I can't think of anything I want more."

"So, you'll marry me?"

"Yes, Mitch, I'll marry you."

"Good," he said, and kissed her. "Soon," he added, lifting his mouth from hers.

"Whenever you want."

The End

Meet The Gallaghers of Montana

Sing Me Back Home
Book 1

Love Me, Cowgirl
Book 2

The Doctor's Christmas Proposal
Book 3

The Cowboy and the Doctor
Book 4

Return of the Cowgirl
Book 5

Available now at your favorite online retailer!

About the Author

Eve Gaddy is the best-selling award-winning author of more than seventeen novels. Her books have won and been nominated for awards from Romantic Times, Golden Quill, Bookseller's Best, Holt Medallion, Texas Gold, Daphne Du Maurier and more. She was nominated for a Romantic Times Career Achievement Award for Innovative Series romance as well as winning the 2008 Romantic Times Career Achievement award for Series Storyteller of the year. Eve's books have sold over a million copies worldwide and been published in many foreign countries. Eve lives in East Texas with her husband of many years.

More from Eve:

Check out her website at EveGaddy.net

Thank you for reading

Return of the Cowgirl

If you enjoyed this book, you can find more from all our great authors at TulePublishing.com, or from your favorite online retailer.

TULE
PUBLISHING

Made in the USA
Monee, IL
25 June 2020

34934022R00134